PRIM WARI DRACU AZUL: FULL METAL CHRONICLES

ANDRES PEREZ

Editing courtesy of Matthew Dennion, Patrick Galvan, David Joshua Hernandez, Dillion McCandless, and Christofer Nigro

Cover Art: Larry Quach

**Cover Formatting: Elden Ardiente of
Lungga Creatives**

Interior Art: Lungga Creatives --

1 Divine Intervention: Ferdie Misa

2 Crossroads: Jimi Bautista

3 A Friend from Afar: Elden Ardiente

4 Reminiscence: Jim Faustino

5 Legacy of Valor: Glenn Lugapo

**6 Bravura - The Wandering Soldier:
Benjamin Quinajon**

Wild Hunt Press

ACKNOWLEDGEMENT

Dedicated to my dearly beloved friend, Christopher Martinez. May his work continue to entertain and inspire future giant monster fans as it has done for me.

GOODBYE, DEAR FRIEND

Art: Tyler Sowles

Dorugan created by Christopher Martinez

Table of Contents

DRACO AZUL: FROM MASCOT TO MYTHOS 1

DRACO AZUL: DIVINE INTERVENTION 7

DRACO AZUL: CROSSROADS 24

DRACO AZUL: A FRIEND FROM AFAR 48

DRACO AZUL: REMINISCENCE 76

DRACO AZUL: LEGACY OF VALOR 105

BRAVURA: THE WANDERING SOLDIER 125

ABOUT THE AUTHOR 150

ABOUT THE ARTISTS 151

DRACO AZUL: FROM MASCOT TO MYTHOS

Forward by Matthew Dennion

Writing a foreword is at the same time both a humbling and a daunting task. On the one hand, someone has considered you both credible enough and knowledgeable enough to write an entry for a literary work. This, of course, entails that you as the foreword writer must be up to the task. In this case, I was asked to write a foreword for Andres Perez's creation: Draco Azul.

Then there is the question about how to approach the foreword. Do I openly admit my personal preferences and biases toward the subject? Or will acting like an impartial observer fit the foreword better? In this case, I feel as if it would be disingenuous of me to try and act like an impartial observer. Despite the fact that I've only met him once face to face, Andres Perez is one of my best friends in the world. So, in this case personal bias on the table.

Now that being said, does this mean that I cannot examine Andres's work with a critical eye? The answer is absolutely not. In fact, because Andres is such a good friend of mine, I am even more inclined to look at his work with a critical eye because I want his work to be the best it can be and, trust me, he would treat me and my work the same way. With all this in mind, let us consider the aspect of the approach to this foreword cleared.

The second question is how to approach the character of Draco Azul itself. Do I start by going over a history of mechs and influences that helped Andres dream up Draco Azul? If so, do I go as far back as Talos in *Jason and the Argonauts* and work my way to *Pacific Rim* listing off mechs? Do I include metallic-skinned warriors like Ultraman and Zone Fighter? I feel as if taking this approach would only serve to tell you, as the reader, about a wide array of characters you already know about and can see their influence on Draco Azul simply by reading this or any other work involving the character.

Thus far we have established that I am Andres's friend and that I am not going to go over a history of mechs. I am sure at this point you are asking, "All right, Matt, so what are you going to do?"

The answer is I am going to explain why I think Draco Azul is a cool and interesting character, and thus by extension why Andres Perez is such an innovative person.

In my opinion, the best fictional characters are those that can be viably represented in numerous ways. For instance, a character like Batman can work great in the campy, corny, cheesy guise of the Adam West Batman (which I love). Or, in the ultra-serious form of the *Dark Knight Returns* Batman. Batman is accessible on a level that can be kid-friendly and comical to adults or as a character that is a commentary on the most serious aspects of society.

The same can be said about Godzilla. He can be the wild and goofy protector we see in *Godzilla vs Megalon* or the nightmarish creature from *The Return of Godzilla*. Either one of these portrayals work, as does everything in between. Let us be honest, though: while we all love Godzilla, when he is portrayed as a serious or horrifying creature there is something inherently comical about two guys in rubber suits engaging in a pro-wrestling style fight standing within a model city.

It is this ability to function on multiple levels that make Draco Azul such an intriguing character. The mighty mech can be whatever Andres needs him to be, while still being considered as a valid representation of the character wherever that need may take him. What is even more amazing is that through Draco Azul, Andres is able to pull this off across multiple forms of media.

Many creators will have one of their characters work as a representation of themselves. It is sort of how they get their own thoughts into a story. This is true for Draco Azul on a metafictional level. The mech champion started out as Andres's mascot for his KaijuNoir channel on YouTube. Draco Azul was literally Andres's mouthpiece to communicate his thoughts to the world. In his original form, Draco Azul was not a representation of Andres. He *was* Andres. Draco Azul was the avatar through which Andres engaged the "People of the Internet," as he calls them.

Starting out with this approach, having an Internet mascot that morphed into a full-fledged character is a brilliant idea. Most people who will read a Draco Azul story already have a concept of who this mech warrior is from his YouTube presence. Moreover, they know who Andres is, and how his personality is infused into Draco Azul. The transformation of Draco Azul from Internet Mascot, to comics, to prose stories is similar to the Shadow's journey from radio mascot to the multimedia phenomenon he would become.

It is interesting that not only does Draco Azul's journey mirror that of the Shadow, but that Andres does a great impersonation of Orson Welles who helped to form the Shadow in his early days. Is this a mere coincidence? I will leave that mystery for you, the reader, to decide.

Back to Draco Azul's journey and versatility. Once Draco Azul was established as Andres's avatar, we began to see how the character could be adapted to fit numerous roles. Aside from the majestic portrayal of Draco Azul we were treated to on numerous title cards, we began to see a Chibi version of the character. More than just being Andres's avatar, this iteration functioned as a full-fledged character in numerous videos with other YouTubers. Most notably with Crookedlore's Augustine and Bell, as well as Brayton Connor.

This was the version of Draco Azul which could dive into the world of comedy and show the humorous side of the genres we all love. With the help of a Crooked Man and a Crooked Cat Girl, the Chibi version of Draco Azul gave us a new incarnation of the character who we could laugh along with, and it also showed us that this blue robot could operate in a story as well as work as an avatar.

Andres would also show us that Draco Azul could walk the line between bringing something which we could enjoy as an escape from reality while also serving to help better the real world in numerous ways. When the Kaiju vs Cancer charity started off, Draco Azul was one of the characters at the heart of the operation and he still is today. As part of the charity the mighty mech would appear on numerous shirts whose profits would go directly to support children fighting cancer.

Andres would then use the Kaiju vs Cancer charity to introduce us to another version of his creation, in the Noir form of Draco Azul. In the short comic *Draco Azul/Atomic Rex: Shadow of the Raptor*, Draco Azul operates as a private investigator in a world where mechs and anthropomorphized kaiju live and work as humans would. Throughout the short story, Andres shows us how in this world, mechs are viewed and treated as second class citizens by the majority of the kaiju. The story is not dominated or driven by this fact, but it is intricately woven into the subtext of the tale.

In a similar fashion to how Stan Lee used the X-Men to make a social commentary on minority groups, Andres was able to do the same with Draco Azul. Aside from the big blue robot providing us with a little subtext on the underbelly of society once more, Draco Azul was able to have a positive effect on the real world as Andres donated all of the proceeds from this comic to help his friend Chris Martinez in his battle with cancer.

The social commentary provided brilliantly by Noir Draco Azul brings us to the version of the character that you will predominantly be reading about in this anthology: The Primal Warrior Draco Azul! This version of the mech is in line with the traditional kaiju-fighting robots that we mentioned earlier like Gundam, Mazinger Z, and those featured in *Pacific Rim*. The version would appear in prose format in the anthology *Courage on Infinite Earths* along with numerous other heroes and mechs (once more the proceeds from this book would go to fight the real-world monster of cancer). The heroic incarnation of the character would also appear in the *Primal Warrior Draco Azul* comic book series.

The Primal Warrior Draco Azul is piloted by Eric Martinez. The robot is an ancient construct given to the Maya civilization by "Strangers from Beyond the Stars" to serve as their protector against giant monsters and other apocalyptic threats.

Eric is a fascinating choice as the pilot of Draco Azul. This is due to the fact that in fiction, most mechs are piloted by characters of Asian, Caucasian, or sometimes African descent. In the long history of mechs, there are only a dozen Power Rangers who are of Hispanic descent of any kind. Most of the time the backgrounds of these Rangers are never brought up.

In a time when children of Hispanic -- in particular, Mexican -- descent see themselves portrayed in the media as anything but heroic and valued, Eric Martinez smashes through the wall around these stereotypes and provides young Hispanic children with a shining example of someone with their heritage acting heroic in a genre that has traditionally been closed to them. As he did with Noir Draco Azul, Andres approaches this subject with nuance and through subtext. First and foremost, Eric Martinez is a hero. His heritage and nationality, while important to him and his character, are not the reason we want to root for him. We want to root for Eric because he is heroic and through that we become more interested in his culture and background.

Eric Martinez comes from the same cloth as well-devised heroes like Buffy the Vampire Slayer, Blade, or Nightwolf from *Mortal Kombat*. We do not feel obligated to root for Buffy because she is a girl, Blade because he is African American, or Nightwolf because he is a Native American. We want to root for them because they are well developed characters, and they kick ass! Eric, like the characters I mentioned as well as numerous others, attract us to them based on their actions. Once we are attached to those characters, we find ourselves more interested to find out about their backgrounds.

In addition to Eric, Andres also introduces us to the AI which lives inside Draco Azul, Ekchuah. Ekchuah is a brilliant commentary on the influence of Native Americans like the Maya on current day Mexican culture. Just as aspects of the Maya culture are interwoven into the people of current day Mexico, so does Ekchuah's teaching influence young Eric. As a whole, Draco Azul represents a wonderful and whimsical peak into the culture of the Mexican people.

So, there you have it. The anthology you now hold in your hands represents a character who works on numerous levels: in the fictional world he is an avatar, a comedy piece, a Noir detective, and a heroic warrior. If you are like me, start hitting up Andres on social media and tell him we want *Into the Dracoverse*! I, for one, would love to see a story where Primal Warrior, Noir, and Chibi Draco Azul are standing side by side.

At the same time you are reading stories about a character whose real world impact includes raising money to help out kids with cancer, raising money to help out a fellow creator with cancer, serving as an inspiration to children (and yes, even adults) whose cultural heritage is sadly underappreciated at this time, and does all this while providing us with an escape from reality.

You may have wondered why I started out stating my biases in regards to Andres Perez when you first read this foreword. I am willing to bet he did too. Not to worry, though; for all the great things I pointed out about Andres, he is a perfectionist. By the time you read this he will have had me reword it at least five times. I just had to point out I am being as objective as possible.

Still, even this serves to show how much thought and effort he puts into his work and his creations.

More importantly, though, I wanted to point out the fact that I do not consider him to be one of my best friends because he is a Mexican American who lives in Japan and has a YouTube channel. I consider one of my best friends because his actions show him to be a caring and dynamic man of impeccable character. I had also mentioned that Andres uses Draco Azul/Eric Martinez/Ekchuah as his mouthpiece and avatar. As such, those same subtle yet endearing qualities -- and yes, in some cases, quirky faults -- that make Andres such a great man are reflected in his characters and his stories.

I hope this foreword has given you some insight as to what you are in for in this book. Enjoy all the cool mech vs monster action that is coming your way, and all the other subtext that is interwoven into those stories.

Matthew Dennion
July 2020

DRACO AZUL: DIVINE INTERVENTION

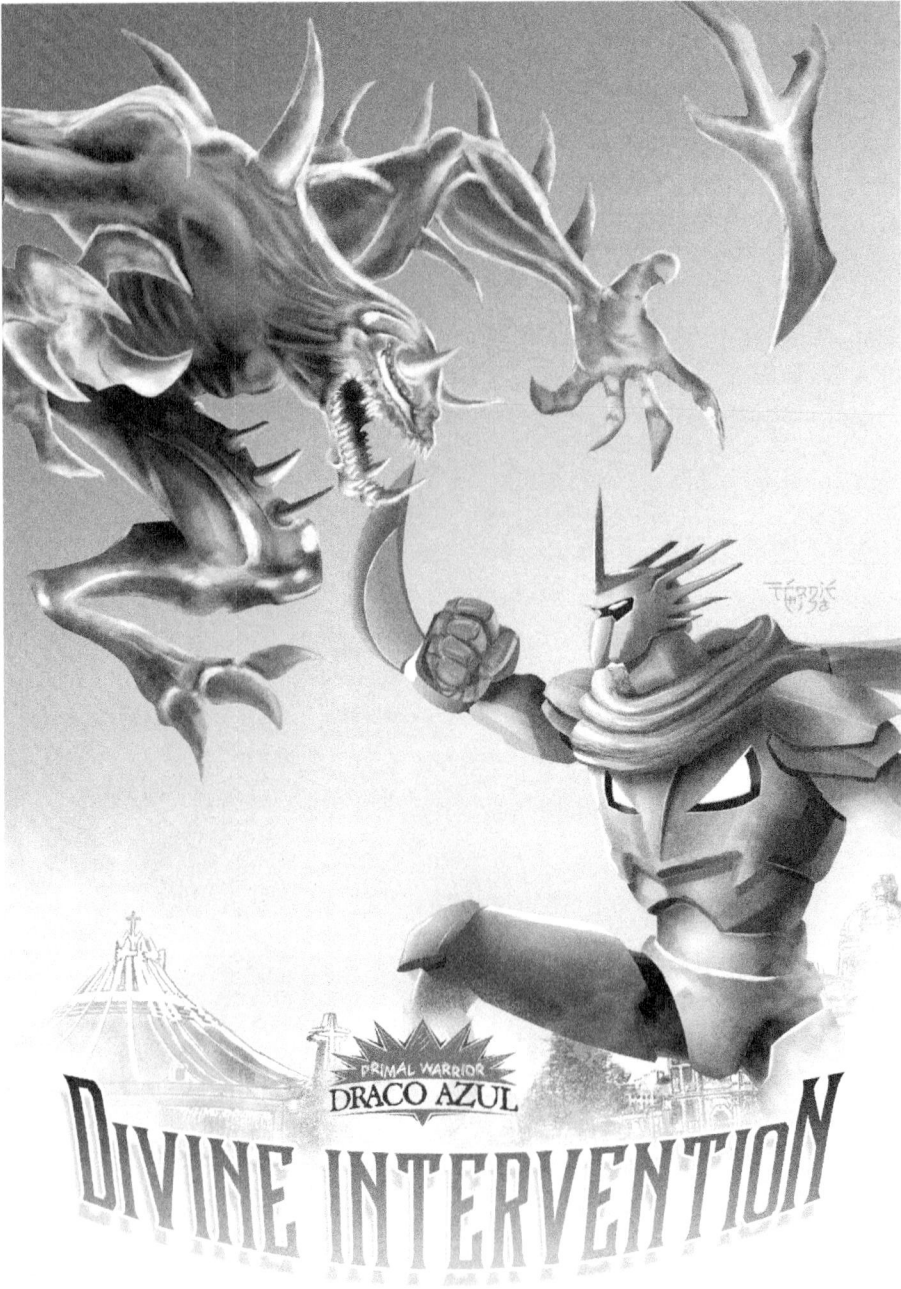

Editor's Note: This yarn is an edited version of the story originally published in the anthology *Courage on Infinite Earths: A Kaiju vs. Cancer Anthology* from the Kaiju vs. Cancer charity label, as well as *Attack of the Kaiju Volume 2: The Next Wave* by Wild Hunt Press.

It was a bright and clear day in the capital of Mexico. However, the sun was not shining on a city filled with peace and prosperity, but one tainted by an unspeakable reign of carnage. For the people of Mexico City, their world was collapsing all around them as a series of black, sludge-like entities appeared out of mysterious otherworldly portals in the center of town. The moment they entered this world their ferocious hunger forced them to consume every organic being in sight. As these things fed on everyone and everything, their mass grew larger, their yellow eyes glowed brighter, and their vicious teeth became sharper.

While the city's population attempted to escape the horror, the military endeavored to intervene. Unfortunately for the humans, the savage invaders had already grown too powerful for their weaponry. Countless bullets, missiles, and grenades were launched at the creatures, only to be proven ineffective as their gelatinous bodies were incapable of being harmed by solid objects and explosives. Every attack launched at the toothy blobs was retaliated with aggression and ferocity. By the time the invasion entered its second hour, the military had to set up a blockade to contain the threat. Sadly, it would take more than a few dozen tanks to hold these demons off.

If anyone outside this scenario were to witness the calamity, they would most likely view this event as the end of days. However, in an ironic twist of fate, this sort of occurrence had been quite common to the people of Mexico. While these invaders were indeed a threat to the country, they were certainly not the first. It was this reason why a champion had arisen to dispel such evil.

Over 200 miles away in the mountainous region of Sierra Madre del Sur, inside a hidden cave, a metal giant lay in slumber. The metallic goliath's yellow eyes lit up and pierced through the darkness. Its body began to move. Standing sixty meters tall, the giant looked towards the entrance of its cave and took its first steps towards it.

Trailing the giant was an elongated, crimson-colored scarf that wrapped around its neck. Its steps quickly picked up speed and within seconds the titan leaped out of the cave. The iron titan's blue and white armor glistened in the sunlight. Just as gravity began to take its toll, a loud voice erupted from the giant.

"Draco Wings!"

Large metal wings sprouted from the giant's back and lifted it into the sky through jet propulsion. The metal warrior was now on its way towards Mexico City. This being was Mexico's, and the world's, last line of defense. *Draco Azul!*

An advanced machine far beyond any sort of human engineering, Draco Azul was given to the Maya civilization centuries ago by what the natives could only describe as "strangers from beyond the stars." These mysterious space Samaritans bestowed upon the Maya people this technological titan to serve as the planet's guardian. For several generations, Draco Azul would protect the world from both earthly and extraterrestrial threats.

However, for reasons unknown, the blue behemoth stayed hidden from the world for the last 800 years, waiting until it was needed once again. In recent times, strange beasts called "Diablos" have threatened the safety of Mexico, which resulted in Draco Azul's resurrection. The ravenous creatures now attacking Mexico City were the latest threat for Draco Azul to vanquish.

However, despite Draco Azul's awesome might, it still required a human spirit to fuel its power. Within the robot's heavily armored chassis was a mortal man, the most recent in a long line of pilots. Throughout history, generations of aeronauts had used Draco Azul as a weapon of justice. The latest individual to take up the mantle was Eric Martinez, a 26-year-old former educator that had reluctantly been tasked with the duty of piloting Draco Azul, having stumbled upon it during the Diablos' initial raid on Cancun.

"How long until we get to Mexico City, coach?" said Eric, as he hovered over his platform facing forward in the same fashion as his flying robot.

The holographic representation of the mech's sophisticated AI system appeared next to the human pilot and activated a screen on the wall of the cockpit. Several statistics were displayed.

Despite his lack of experience in fighting, Eric had become a very quick learner thanks in part to the AI system that ran the majority of Draco Azul's functions. This AI was Ekchuah, named by the Maya people after their god of travelers and journeys. In the case of *this* Ekchuah, he would guide previous pilots on a journey of dedication, bravery, and heroism. Out of respect for the people who first adopted Draco Azul, he took on the appearance of a Maya warrior via his hologram avatar.

It was through Ekchuah's assistance that Eric grew accustomed to Draco Azul's control mechanisms, an astounding system that allowed the robot's movements to follow his. By standing on a platform while wearing the necessary bodysuit and accessories, Eric could feel the sensation of having the body of a god.

"At our speed, we'll be there in about twenty minutes. We could get there in ten, but it's gonna cost us more fuel," Ekchuah explained.

"I see. How much would we have by then?" Eric replied.

"Depends on how we'll fight these things. We'll be okay if we stick to physical combat. Though if you plan to really dish out the pain, you'll only have enough left over for one big shot."

Draco Azul's systems ran on the electrostatic discharges provided by Earth's thunderstorms, with the mech's horn acting as an immense lightning rod. It had been a while since the giant last replenished its power due to the fact that thunderstorms weren't as common this time of year.

Eric paused for a moment, thinking about the immeasurable amount of suffering the victims of Mexico City must be experiencing.

"Alright, set boosters to full speed."

Ekchuah smiled. "That's what I like to hear, kid!"

Draco Azul's wings propelled the mech even faster than before -- from the speed of an air carrier to that of a jet fighter. As the robot passed each city, hundreds of men, women, and children alike could hear the azure goliath soar through the sky. To them, it was as if they were listening to the screech of a mighty dragon. They all knew that their mysterious hero was on the move, ready to save more unfortunate souls.

As Draco Azul approached the perimeters of the city, Eric saw a large swarm of the black monsters converging on one location. Others were attacking the tanks that reinforced the blockade. Eric's eyes darted all around the battlefield as he was making a dive.

"Hey coach, find the best place to land."

"Already on it!"

In mere seconds, red and green dots appeared in Eric's field of vision. Many of the green points were centered around a spot Eric recognized from his childhood. Around this collection was a ring of red dots closing in.

"The red points are the enemies; I've counted 86 of them. The green ones are the civilians still inside the area. As you can see, many of the enemies are near the blockades, most likely trying to escape. However, a large group of them are circling around the biggest gathering of civilians. Which is—"

"The Basilica of Guadalupe!"

"Yeah. You familiar with it?"

"Of course! It's practically the holiest place in the Americas! No wonder everyone's there."

"All the more reason to land there and, hopefully, attract the vermin at the blockade."

"You don't have to tell me twice!"

"Of course not, kid. Now, let's show these bastards who's boss!"

Eric aimed his mech feet-first at the group of the black creatures farthest from the Basilica. He knew he was not going to let these demons hurt any more people. Draco Azul landed with a thunderous boom as the ground beneath its feet caved in, crushing the monsters underneath the metal giant into black puddles.

The cockpit Eric stood in gave him the benefit of being in whatever position Draco Azul found itself thanks to its gyroscopic design. If the mech were to fall on its back, Eric would find himself doing the same within his cockpit despite the rest of the mech laying down.

Whatever happened, the cockpit would remain parallel to the ground.

Nearly every remaining creature turned around to face their challenger. Their eyes glowed intensely as they all screamed in unison.

The invaders started crawling towards the mech. Eric held up his arms, as did Draco Azul in unison, showing off its razor-sharp arm blades. As the swarm approached, he took a few steps back so as to bring the battle farther away from the Basilica. He could see through his mech's telescopic vision that the church was in the clear. The young pilot breathed a slight sigh of relief. With one hand, he performed the sign of the cross.

"Hm, never pegged you as the religious type," Ekchuah proclaimed with a hint of amused curiosity.

Eric rarely, if ever, practiced his mother's Catholicism once he reached his teens, but that did not mean that he didn't believe in the existence of a higher power. Plus, with the recent appearances of Draco Azul and unearthly monstrosities such as these, he figured anything was possible. So, if there was a God up there, he thanked the Lord that the people were safe… for now. Eric opened his eyes, focused and ready to fight.

"Let's do this!"

Draco Azul rushed towards the approaching horrors. Many of them assimilated into one another to form larger blobs of slime. They all came at the mech like huge black whips, barbed with thousands of sharp teeth. This did not deter Eric as he swung his arms at each of these assailing masses, cleaving all of them in two. In the process, he had also stepped on the smaller monsters like the vermin they were.

Draco Azul paused as soon as it ran through the army. The goliath quickly turned around, its back facing the Basilica. The mech was now the only thing standing between the monsters and the majority of the survivors.

To Eric's shock, he noticed that his attacks left no lasting damage on the strange life forms. The monsters slowly reformed and had begun to assimilate into a single, giant abomination. Even the creatures within the crater Draco Azul made with its landing were joining in… as were the reinforcements from the perimeter of the border. Sweat poured down Eric's head. He turned to his AI companion.

"This ain't good."

"Good? Since when was it *ever* good?"

"Got a point there. Any suggestions?"

"Well, we could use our strongest move, but I can't guarantee it'll wipe them all out in one fell swoop. But we still have another ace up our sleeve: the Draco Kick!"

Eric's eyes widened in shock.

"What?"

Ekchuah smirked as if he was excited by his own plan.

"Rather than risk blasting our opponent into a million pieces, we'll electrocute the whole thing from the inside out!"

"B-but I dunno if I can pull it off. I just started practicing last week!"

"Trust me, kid, you got what it takes."

The smile on Ekchuah's face somewhat alleviated Eric's concerns. His mentor was always demanding, but at the same time understanding of the pilot's limitations as a fighter. Before he accidentally stumbled across Ekchuah and Draco Azul, Eric Martinez was merely a high school social studies teacher in southern California. Getting into confrontations, let alone actual fights, was the last thing he ever wanted. However, all it took was a trip to Cancun, and a lot of bad luck, which landed him in a position that required him to change his pacifistic outlook on life. He had learned to throw caution to the wind and fight for what he felt was right.

As the newly assimilated beast howled into the sky, Eric thought about the people hiding in the Basilica and how they must be praying for mercy. He thought about the Mexican soldiers fighting to protect the blockade from what few creatures remained at the perimeter. He thought about the innumerable people already killed. Most importantly, he thought about how far this destruction would spread if he were to fail. With a newfound sense of vengeance burning within, Eric knew that his only option was to face the invader.

The singular entity had finished its metamorphosis. Its body no longer had an intangible appearance, but rather a solid structure. It had grown arms, legs, and a head in an attempt to imitate its opponent. However, it had twisted and contorted its body into an animalistic form, complete with a lengthy barbed tail. Its hunched back was rigid with spines, identical to its teeth. In fact, its whole body was covered with them. Its head, torso, limbs, and tail were adorned with these razor-sharp protrusions. The beast opened its three glowing eyes and focused them on Draco Azul. Eric remained undeterred and raised his fists once more.

Ekchuah chuckled to himself. "Heh, it may be bigger, but now it made itself one giant target. Makes our job a whole lot easier. Keep its attention on you, kid, and wait until I give the signal."

"Got it, coach!"

The beast slammed its hands to the ground and began to charge at the blue robot. The monster lunged at the mech bearing every one of its teeth and claws. With perfect timing, Draco Azul countered with an uppercut into the creature's mouth with its blade slicing through its torso in the process. The monster fell on its back, only for it to restlessly get back up.

Draco Azul retaliated with several more jabs and swings. However, once the blade-wielding mech stepped back Eric noticed that every gash on the demon's body slowly reformed to its original shape. The intrepid pilot was *really* ticked off now.

"Well, that rules out a beat down," an annoyed Eric stated.

"Yeah, but at least we know it's not as tough as it looks. Continue to hold it off!"

Just then the beast's central eye glowed fiercely as its head finished healing. With an intense roar, the monster fired a concentrated beam of yellow energy at Draco Azul. Eric quickly placed his hands up and endured the full force of the blast. As much as his arms ached, he knew that if he moved away from his spot, the Basilica was as good as gone. Suddenly, Eric heard Ekchuah's voice.

"Eric, look out!"

Eric peeked from beyond his robot's arms and witnessed numerous claws coming at him from both sides. Draco Azul leaped backward just as the two sets of talons closed in on each other like a Venus flytrap. Unfortunately, the Primal Warrior's agility was not quick enough as the claws dug into the sides of its torso, leaving deep gashes as it escaped their grasp. Excruciating pain surged through Eric.

Through Eric's suit, he could experience Draco Azul's vision, its power... and its torment. Any time Draco Azul was damaged, Eric would feel an approximation of the blows given to his mech. Ekchuah once explained that this sensation was made to heighten the user's senses, as well as increase their urgency if Draco Azul was ever in critical condition. After all, how could you fight with one disabled arm if your natural body still thought it could use two?

Eric looked up and noticed that the attacking claws came from the monster's chest, which had morphed into a sideways mouth. Had he not moved out of the way at the last possible second, things could have gotten ugly. Ekchuah then created a map of the war zone and displayed it on Eric's visor.

"We're a lot closer to the church now. Take extra caution!" the hologram advised in a stern tone.

Eric realized that things had to end here and now. Just as the beast was about to attack, Draco Azul made the first move and started rushing towards the monster. The creature screeched as it prepared for another assault. However, this time the machine jumped over the beast. Once Draco Azul landed behind it, the monster turned around -- only for it to realize that its opponent's scarf was now wrapped around it.

With Eric's diversion successful, he made his mech grab its scarf and pull the monster towards him and further away from the Basilica. The creature then dug its feet and tail into the ground as it struggled to free its arms and legs.

"Draco Wings!"

With quick thinking, Eric had Draco Azul activate its wings once more through his vocal command. The moment they sprung forth from its back, the mech blasted off into the air.

The lassoed beast was yanked out from the ground and was now trailing behind the metal titan. In desperation, the monster made its body intangible and began traveling up Draco Azul's scarf. In response, Ekchuah flashed a warning on Eric's visor with footage from the mech's external cameras.

"Heads up, kid!"

With quick thinking, Eric made Draco Azul dive straight downward while loosening his scarf's grip on his opponent. With its body still forced into an upwards projection, the invader completely slid off the mech's scarf. Eventually, gravity started working against the abomination. The beast flailed its tentacles in all directions in a failed attempt to grab onto anything to stop its descent.

At this point, it had all but abandoned its solid form save for its head. After a few seconds, the monster smashed into the middle of the city, creating another massive crater. Within the massive puddle of black sludge, its horrific head reformed and roared in anger. Every single creature that was once trying to escape the area was now heading towards the larger entity. As the last of the invaders assimilated into the main beast, the head looked all around for its enemy.

Suddenly, a bright light shined overhead. The invader looked up and saw crackling arcs of electricity. Miles above the monster, Draco Azul was summoning forth the last of its expendable energy. Bolts of lightning surged from his horn. The mecha-warrior then raised its right knee and transferred the energy into its leg.

"Now, kid! Bring the pain!"

Draco Azul's wings activated their reverse thrusters and blasted the giant robot downward foot first. While the mech was descending towards the monster, Eric began to recite the name of his hidden ace, activating it in the process.

"Dracoooo…"

The giant's robotic boot that was once surging with lightning was now enveloped by the glow of the raw, concentrated power. Draco Azul's path of descent was now highlighted with sparks of excess lightning bursting from its foot. Eric finished reciting his attack, which became his declaration of victory.

"Kiiiiiiiiiick!"

The beast had realized what was approaching, but it was too late. It had not finished fully assimilating back into a mobile form and there wasn't enough time to completely separate and escape the deep crater. Like a cornered animal, its only instinct was to fight back. The monster quickly created several tentacles adorned with as many teeth-spikes it could muster and launched them at the attacking metal warrior.

Draco Azul's foot came crashing down on the monster's tentacles, each disintegrating within seconds. The mech landed a kick into the beast's face with all its might. The monster let out a loud but truncated screech before its reign of terror came to an end. Draco Azul's foot pierced through the creature's head and entered the deepest pit of the semi-solid monstrosity's gelatinous body.

By then the lighting had begun to evaporate the disgusting matter that composed the creature faster than it could create new appendages to counter the offense. Some pieces of the monster attempted to separate from the main body. Luckily, however, the energy from Draco Azul's attack expanded all throughout the deepening crater, taking with it every last bit of the black sludge.

Miles away, the residents of Mexico City had already begun to exit the Basilica. To their shock, they witnessed what seemed like an act of God, as they saw what looked like a massive bolt of lightning falling onto the demon that tried to kill them all. The resulting impact took down several more city blocks with it. Many had hoped this would bring an end to the disaster. Others hoped that their mysterious savior would be alright. Some tried to look away from the unimaginable levels of destruction that not even Mother Nature could create.

A few moments later, Eric recovered from the attack and managed to catch his breath. He opened his eyes and noticed that the area around him had widened up. The young aviator looked down and beheld the charred remains of the sludge that once threatened the very existence of North America. He quickly turned to Ekchuah.

"Any casualties?"

"Nope. You managed to get that thing far enough from the locals. See for yourself!"

Back at the Basilica men, women, and children all came outside after they heard the lightning's crackle subside. Their eyes lit up as they gazed upon the blue and white robot exiting the crater with its scarf billowing in the wind. They had all cheered, and some of them thanked God for blessing them with such a hero. Others quickly embraced their families and loved ones, grateful that they managed to survive the nightmare and lived to see another day.

Draco Azul's telescopic vision allowed Eric to confirm that the people were all right. He wished he could have avoided causing more damage to the city. Though at this point, he took whatever satisfaction he could get at a time like this. He let out a long sigh of relief.

"Whew! It's over. For now, at least."

"Don't celebrate too quickly, kid. Ya did good, but there's still the problem of that thing back there."

Eric was confused. What was Ekchuah talking about? He looked back at the pile of ashes that used to be the black creature. The holographic AI system brought up microscopic scans on Eric's visor. There the young man could see that within the ashes something survived.

"While the activity in that black matter subsided, its cells are still alive… somewhat."

"Dammit! Well, what *can* we do?"

Draco Azul approached the gray dust to take a closer look at it. The AI-driven hologram pondered as he attempted to determine its genetic makeup.

"Let's see… I tell ya, this thing's one tough nut to crack. I can't make heads or tails of it. It's like it –"

"Came from another dimension?"

This foreign voice sent a shock through Eric as he had never heard anyone other than Ekchuah within his cockpit.

"Gah!"

The pilot ripped the visor off his head, and to his surprise, he found the most bizarre figure standing mere feet away from him and Ekchuah's hologram. The male figure was a head taller than him and had a slender build. The stranger wore a blue and orange coat and top hat, like a neon-colored 18th-century gentleman.

That alone was bizarre, but to top off this otherworldly sight was the figure's face. It appeared to be wearing a mask. The right half was white and had a toothy grin, while the other was black with a depressing frown. The being talked through the right half of his mask.

"I'm sorry, did I come at a bad time?"

Eric did not pay attention to the stranger's smug apology. He was too freaked out to care.

"Who... *what* the hell are you?"

Meanwhile, Ekchuah's hologram waved his hand, activating the cockpit's defense mechanisms. The room's lights turned on and two mechanical arms ending in tasers extended from the walls.

"You better start talking, fella. One wrong move and you're done!"

The skeletal figure chuckled to himself and bowed towards the duo out of an ironic sense of courtesy.

"Heh heh heh. Oh, where are my manners? Allow me to introduce myself. I'm Augustine, though my victims call me the *Crookedman*. I came here to assist you with that abomination you just faced, but it seemed you had a handle on things. So, I decided to sit back and watch you guys do your thing."

Ekchuah's hologram raised an eyebrow at the sarcastic Crookedman.

"Hold on. You mean to tell me you've been *here* the whole time? How did I not pick you up? I can see everything here."

Eric stepped in between the Crookedman and the holographic avatar of the mech's AI system.

"Unless... you *chose* not to let us see you."

The Crookedman's crooked smile grew even more devilish.

"Bingo! This guy definitely gets the idea!"

Ekchuah rubbed his chin.

"So, you're from another dimension, eh? Shame my creators never filled me in on guys like you. Guess they never thought Earthlings would have to deal with extradimensional threats. Either that or they weren't aware of beings like you and that monster."

The Crookedman now spoke from the frowning side of his face.

"Hey, don't you start comparing me to that mindless beast!"

Eric raised his voice in an attempt to show authority.

"Did you send that monster here? Are you responsible for all this?"

The Crookedman switched back to talking through the smiling half.

"Ha! Please. If I wanted to kill, maim, and torture an entire city I would've done it myself. Besides, killing mortals on a grand scale isn't really my style. I'm more of the Faustian kind of guy."

Eric and Ekchuah stood silent. The Crookedman's eyes shifted back and forth between the two of them and decided to continue.

"Y'know the whole 'deal-with-the-devil' business? Yeah, that's my thing. And unfortunately, some interdimensional jackass is taking all that away from me! So, I and a mortal from a universe different from this one decided to find some people who can help deal with the problem."

Ekchuah crossed his arms and spoke.

"And you think Draco Azul can help you."

"Exactly! I'm fairly certain you guys got the chops. After all, you already took down one of the creature's children."

Eric's heart skipped a beat. "Children...?"

"Oh yeah, this thing's merely a piece of the real deal. Now, a calamity this large doesn't occur very often. So, if it's any consolation, this is the first time I've ever seen one personally. And I've been around for several centuries."

Ekchuah remained unenthused with the Crookedman's demeanor.

"It's not. So, if we help you then our universe will be safe?"

"Yes, as well as the rest of reality. So, you, me, and everyone else can continue doing what we do best."

Another moment of silence passed. Eric and Ekchuah looked at each other. The hologram then approached the Crookedman.

"How can we believe that anything you say is true?"

The Crookedman closed his eyes and shrugged.

"Well, for starters, I already took care of the dust pile you left behind. So, you won't have to worry about that thing coming back."

Eric looked at Ekchuah. His holographic ally nodded and activated a monitor on the wall, displaying Draco Azul's POV camera. Indeed, every trace of the creature was gone. This confounded Eric.

"Where'd you put it?"

"Oh, don't worry about that. I sent it somewhere where it'll never bother anyone again. Now, I heard about your little 'fuel problem.' How about we make a deal? I refill your robot's tank, and you'll assist me in saving the multiverse!"

Ekchuah grew even more skeptical.

"And *how* exactly are you gonna do that?"

At that moment, the entire mech was enveloped in a shroud of black mist. The Crookedman's eyes took on a reddish glow as he spoke with a louder and echoing voice through both halves of his face.

"Oh, I thought you'd never ask!"

The entire room shook as if there was an earthquake. Eric grabbed onto the wall of his cockpit to keep himself from falling. Meanwhile, Ekchuah attempted to tase the Crookedman, only for the electro-shock wires to phase harmlessly through him.

"Ha! Silly old program. Your tech may be impressive, but it's not enough to bring down the Crookedman!" Augustine boasted.

The cockpit suddenly stopped shaking and loud thunderous booms could be heard outside. The Crookedman's manner of speaking returned to normal.

"Ah, we're here!"

Eric and Ekchuah looked at the monitor as they saw that Draco Azul was now standing in a river with hundreds of lightning bolts covering the sky! The first of several bolts struck Draco Azul's horn and the mech quickly began converting its energy into fuel. Eric was astounded by the sight.

"Where are we?"

The Crookedman responded with great enthusiasm. "This is the Catatumbo River in Venezuela, the best place for all your lightning needs! It was the best I could do on such short notice."

Within minutes, Draco Azul was fully restored to its full strength with enough left over to fill its extra reserves. Ekchuah still was not impressed.

"Big deal! We could've come here ourselves. What makes you think we could trust you?"

"Oh, you don't have to. You just need to hold up your end of the deal."

Eric stepped in. "But we never agreed to it!"

The Crookedman grinned. "I know, and that's why I'm going to leave you stranded elsewhere, away from any other source of power with zero fuel, *unless* you agree to help me save the multiverse."

Eric and Ekchuah looked at each other with concern. With his back against the wall, Eric once more thought about the fate of his world. Ekchuah could read the contemplative look on his protégé's face. The holographic avatar nodded to him with assurance. Eric turned to face their vexing adversary.

"Alright, we'll do it. But once this is over, you'll send us back here right away!"

Ekchuah placed his hands on his hips and sighed. "You really are a crooked sonuvagun."

Augustine winked. "Why, thank you. I do my best!"

As if on cue the cockpit started vibrating once more. The Crookedman grew even more excited.

"Now, let's get down to business. Team Draco, prepare to *roll out!*"

An awkward silence took place between the three of them. Eric facepalmed. If what the young man thought was true, he could not believe their crooked guest made that reference at a time like this. At the same time, Ekchuah was completely lost. Their new ally grew annoyed with their reactions and shrugged.

"Hey, that was better than 'it's morphin' time,' am I right?"

Once Eric and Ekchuah collectively rolled their eyes at the Crookedman's comments, the otherworldly phantom turned away from the two and began to talk to himself.

"Now, let's hope Bell got ahold of *her* favorite mech. If she did, we might actually survive this little escapade…"

END

Editor's note: If you're interested in seeing where this story leads and where the sludge-like monsters came from, be sure to get yourself a copy of the multi-author crossover anthology *Courage on Infinite Earths: A Kaiju vs. Cancer Anthology*. All proceeds to that publication from the Kaiju vs. Cancer charity label go to St. Jude Children's Hospital to help wage war against childhood cancer! An

earlier version of this story appeared there, along with many other super-hero stories from a variety of authors.

Augustine the Crookedman and Bell the Crooked Catgirl were created by and are copyright William T. Kearney. You can see more of them on the Crookedlore Productions YouTube channel.

DRACO AZUL: CROSSROADS

Deep within the mountainous region of Sierra Madre del Sur, Mexico, existed an undiscovered cave hidden from the world. Within this secret cave was a massive mechanical giant of extraterrestrial origin. This behemoth of a machine was slumped over in a sitting position, its back leaning against the ancient wall. Despite its seemingly lifeless appearance, the mech had seen plenty of action over the past several months.

Mexico was in the middle of an invasion of cataclysmic proportions, and it was because of this robot that the denizens of Mexico continued to live comfortable, albeit cautious lives. However, this was not all the robot's doing, for it was not an autonomous guardian. Inside the mech lay the man behind the machine. The person who wielded the power of an entire thunderstorm. His name was Eric Martinez and his only weapon against the beasts that beckoned his call was the mighty Draco Azul. Yet, for the man who seemingly had the power to overcome every obstacle that came his way, there was one particular hurdle he had trouble overcoming: isolation.

Initially, Eric had come to this country as a means of escaping his mundane life, if only temporarily. Yet, little did this everyman knew, he was trading in his thankless and monotonous job for one full of destruction, violence, and peril. It was at this time that the invasion began in Cancun, Mexico. There, a trio of mysterious beasts (*Diablos* to the public) emerged from the ground and attacked the city. However, the chaos was swiftly put to an end by the sheer strength of the metallic hero the public had dubbed "Draco Azul." For Eric Martinez, this was the day that changed his life forever.

Though this was not how he envisioned his stay in Mexico would be, deep down inside Eric knew this was his responsibility the moment he first discovered the mechanical humanoid hidden deep underneath the ruins of Chichén Itzá. Perhaps it was fate that led him to Draco Azul's sleeping chambers; perhaps it was sheer coincidence that an average joe stumbled upon such a discovery. Whatever the case was, be it an accident or some divine calling, he was at the right place at the right time for the people of Mexico.

Since that fateful night, Eric had defended Mexico again and again, learning the ins and outs of his mech in the process. The young man had been at this for some time now and had gotten accustomed to wielding Draco Azul's raw strength. Though recently, he had encountered an absurdly long period of downtime. Normally, during this period the pilot would occupy his time with further training, studying recordings of his previous battles, or overlooking Draco Azul's auto-repair systems. Yet after performing today's regiment, he found himself lying in his cockpit's fold-out bed and staring at the ceiling. It was at this point that he realized something: he had not been outside in what felt like an eternity.

Indeed, Eric had been so preoccupied with keeping Mexico safe and remaining ever vigilant that at no point did he think to leave the safety of his robot and interact with the outside world he fought so hard to protect. After all, all he could ever need was conveniently available within Draco Azul's chassis.

Draco Azul was truly an extraordinary machine. Countless centuries prior, at the height of the Maya Empire, a mysterious race of extraterrestrial beings chose Earth as a planet worthy of their protection. Admiring the Maya for their accomplishments in art, culture, mathematics, and astronomy, they had created a protector they themselves could utilize to preserve their world from apocalyptic catastrophes. Upon learning of these space beings from Draco Azul's translated records, Eric had since dubbed them "The Samaritans," after the Biblical parable.

Upon becoming the latest human to pilot the azure titan, Eric had discovered that this mech was designed to sustain its pilot for a variety of situations. This included all the basic necessities for survival. Draco Azul had a built-in filtration system to provide its pilot with enough clean oxygen and water and could store an emergency supply specifically for environments where none existed, including the vacuum of space.

Directly behind the cockpit was another room where Eric took residence. Here, he could comfortably acquire rest from the bed he rested on that folded out from the wall, as well as nourishment from the refrigerator right beside him. This device stored an obscene amount of nonperishable food of indeterminable origin: food that could refuel his body with the strength needed to continue onward with his mission.

Opposite to the fridge on the other side of the room was the bathroom compartment. This third more compact room contained a shower for decontamination, all the amenities needed for keeping oneself sanitized, and a toilet for purposes that do not necessarily require explanation yet are equally necessary for one to cleanse themselves.

Indeed, there was no real logical reason Eric needed to leave the robot when he had everything he could possibly need, save for an extra change of clothing beyond his pilot suit and street clothes. Yet, Eric had missed the luxuries most would take for granted, such as fresh air and human interaction. He was also getting sick of seeing the same three rooms and eating the same bland, bizarre alien food. He was also beginning to experience claustrophobia from sitting around doing nothing when a Diablo wasn't on the attack.

I really need a change in scenery, thought Eric. *I'm losing my mind in here!* That was when he called out to the closest thing he had to a friend.

"Hey, Ekchuah!"

At that moment, the holographic form of a bare-chested man in traditional Maya warrior garb materialized before Eric's eyes. The collection of lights was projected by sensors on the ceiling so as to display this individual anywhere within Draco Azul at any time. This being that Eric was addressing was Ekchuah, the artificial intelligence program that runs most of Draco Azul's functions. In other words, he was the literal heart and mind of Draco Azul.

Centuries ago, the Samaritans had created Ekchuah to act as a mentor for each pilot that took the reins of piloting the robot. Over time he was named after the Maya god of travelers as he guided each of his pupils to victory. The moment Eric had activated Draco Azul, he was met by Ekchuah, who quickly learned his language via the mech's advanced wireless connection to humanity's recent invention: the World Wide Web. From there on out, Ekchuah sought to whip the young man into shape to become Earth's latest savior.

"Whaddya need, kid?" The hologram asked.

"Think I could take a break?" Eric queried. "Maybe hit the town? I swear, I'm going nuts just laying around here!"

"Have you gone over Draco's systems? Checked up on the calibrations and recordings?"

"Yeah, yeah," said an annoyed Eric.

"How about you? You already ate? Did your workout?"

"Yes! I've done all of that. Now can we take Draco out somewhere?"

Ekchuah crossed his arms. He was known to do this whenever he felt hesitant. Despite being made of ones and zeroes, he thought and acted like a real human being. It was times like this where Eric would forget that Ekchuah was not an actual living person.

"I don't know, kid," Ekchuah responded. "Taking Draco Azul out on anything other than missions could be dangerous for the public. Let's say you do take him out. Where do you expect to keep him?"

Eric paused for a moment. Then suddenly, a thought came to him.

"Underwater! Near a small town."

"Hmm, that could work."

"Awesome. It's settled then-"

"Where?" Ekchuah abruptly asked.

"What?"

"Where do you wanna go? I can't give my approval unless I know we can remain outta sight. I've seen how people would react to Draco in my day and trust me, these folks today ain't ready to see a sixty-meter robot strolling over them."

Eric pondered where his destination could be. As much as he missed home back in the States, he did not want to go beyond Mexico's borders. As far as he knew, the Diablos were only concerned with this portion of land, for whatever reason. He had also seen the reports via Draco Azul's feed that the USA was strengthening its borders in response to the Diablos' presence. Having Draco near or beyond the border would only cause a massive panic from both sides.

Creating an international crisis was the last thing Eric wanted. Still, he figured the next best thing was to get as close as possible without alarming any military officials. Then it hit him.

"Ensenada?"

Ekchuah raised his hand and opened a holographic screen showcasing a map of the coastal city in Baja California. He scanned through the whole location before turning to Eric.

"Keep Draco away from the Navy and near the mountains and we should be good. Also, let's travel underwater. It'll be more discreet."

Within moments Eric had sprung up, quickly donned his pilot suit, and applied the attachments needed for activating Draco Azul. The moment all systems were online, the gargantuan mech's eyes illuminated the whole cave and began to rise. Mimicking all of Eric's movements, Draco Azul ran towards the entrance of the cave. The metal goliath launched itself over the edge of the cliff. Just as it was about to descend, Eric shouted.

"Draco Wings!"

Two large fins extended from its back through the power of its nanotechnology. These jet-fueled appendages propelled Draco Azul through the sky. After a few minutes, the blue behemoth had already reached the shores of the Pacific Ocean and dived right into the water. Within the cockpit, Ekchuah activated the marine settings for Draco Azul's wings, trading in its jet propulsion for electrically charged propellers. Finally, Eric was on his way towards Ensenada.

As the duo began their journey towards the city, Ekchuah turned his attention away from the main screen showcasing Draco Azul and Eric's shared vision.

"So, Ensenada, huh? Are ya homesick?"

This caught Eric by surprise.

"W-what?"

"It's natural, kid. I've worked with a few guys back then who missed their families whenever we were away for too long."

"Well, it's not that. I want to see what's going on in SoCal. I obviously can't go there, and TJ's too close to the border. So... this is the next best thing."

Ekchuah chuckled to himself.

"Heh, I see now. Just wanna be somewhere familiar, eh?"

"Pretty much. Plus, I heard about Ensenada a few times back home. Figured this'll be a better chance than any."

As Eric returned his focus towards the destination ahead, he began to think about home. Eric never had much of a social life, so he doubted anyone who was remotely close to him had noticed his disappearance by now. He was also not very close to his family either, especially his father after his parents' divorce. He never told either of them that he was going to Mexico and he certainly did not want to worry anyone by calling them now.

In fact, the only people who would immediately notice his absence would be the faculty at the school he worked at. By now, all of his vacation days had long been spent. He imagined he must have lost his job by now. Unless, however, he was presumed missing or dead as a result of the Diablos since he had told the principal where he was going prior to leaving.

As Eric reflected on his life prior to becoming Draco Azul's pilot, he was beginning to think that perhaps things have not changed all that much between now and then. He was still stuck with a role he was not fully prepared for and only accepted out of obligation. Nothing much beyond that.

Eric shook his head and began to focus on Ensenada, a place where he could better clear his head and make sense out of what his life had become.

At that moment, the colossal form of Draco Azul skimmed over what appeared to be a smooth mound of sand. The force of the titan's speed blew over the layers of sand that laid on top of the structure, revealing a deep blue-green hill. However, Draco Azul was moving far too fast for Eric and Ekchuah to notice this and the object was not alerting Draco Azul's security systems due to its immobile presence.

By the time the robot was at a safe enough distance, the mound began to move…

***

After several hours of admiring the oceanic view, Eric caught a glimpse on his radar and found that his goal was finally in sight. Ekchuah reaffirmed his thoughts.

"Ah good, looks like we're here. Let's move over to the Punta Banda Peninsula. On the way here I read about a pretty neat geyser in the area that people visit called La Bufadora. That oughta be a decent place for some R&R."

A smile formed on Eric's face. He was not sure if Ekchuah's actions were predetermined by his programming or if he cared for his well-being as would an actual person. Either way, he was grateful to have someone like Ekchuah in his life.

"Thanks, coach."

Ekchuah chuckled. "Don't mention it. I may not be human, but I have a grasp on what people like to do for fun. I took my past trainees all over this land; heck, all over the *world!* Though we had to be pretty discreet back in the day. Nowadays, it's impossible for this giant hunk of metal to do so when everyone on the planet's capable of instantly capturing and sharing images wirelessly!"

Eric rolled his eyes as Ekchuah was going into another one of his long-winded speeches about the "good ol' days." Ekchuah could see Eric not paying attention as his pupil commanded the mech to move ever so slightly towards the rocky hills of a coastline devoid of people.

"Look, kid," Ekchuah said as he tried to get his protégé's attention. "Bottom line is this. Since we're not on a mission, we're gonna have to keep Draco Azul submerged once you're on land. So, to keep in touch, I'm gonna give you this."

Eric took off his helmet and his suit began to disassemble piece by piece. As he changed into his old t-shirt and jeans, he noticed Ekchuah raising his hand over the ground in front of him. On the floor, a rectangular pillar sprouted. The top of the pillar opened to reveal a blue device. As it raised to Eric's chest level Ekchuah began to explain the device's purpose.

"This here is a communicator that you can use to contact me and vice-versa. Its signal strength covers a 500 square mile area, which gives you a lotta leeway as to how far you can be from Draco. If duty calls, I'll contact you. Or, if you're in a pinch, you can program a specific command that'll automatically activate all of Draco's systems. At that point, I'll bring the mech over to your location."

"H-hopefully we won't need to do that," Eric said with a sense of uneasiness in his voice. "But in case we do, what do I say?"

"That's your call, kid. All the other pilots wanted to have their own commands, so I'd reprogram the device each time. Tell you what, I'll let you decide when the right phrase comes to you. Personally, if ya ask me it should be something big and dramatic! Just shout it out and the device will instantly save it."

"On top of that," he added, "the Draco Communicator, DraCom for short, can provide GPS functionalities. So, you'll never get lost."

Eric reached out and grabbed the device. He noticed that its blue color and appearance matched that of Draco Azul's draconian chest. It looked like a wristwatch, so he instinctively placed it on his left arm. The communicator clamped onto his hand and tightened to a comfortable level. Finally, the dragon-like eyes glowed, indicating that it was ready for use. Eric looked over to Ekchuah, who was manipulating a pair of mechanical arms from the ceiling to bring him a metal canister within a small pouch with a strap.

"You probably don't have a lot of money left on ya. So, take this… it's from the fridge and it'll provide you enough nutrients to last the day."

"A day? Just how long do you think I'll be out?" exclaimed a surprised Eric.

Ekchuah smirked, raised his hands, and shrugged.

"Hey, if ya need anything else you know where we are."

Eric was not sure whether to take that as a snarky remark or genuine advice. Then again, he never stated exactly how long he wanted to stay out. Even he did not know at that very moment. He only wanted to be outside again.

"Well… thanks."

The doors in front of Draco Azul's chest slid open and the afternoon light pierced the cockpit. The scent of saltwater filled the room along with a light coastal breeze. Already, Eric's heart was racing with anticipation.

From the opening of the cockpit, he could see a rocky ledge. A flat metal walkway extended from the cockpit's opening and connected to the ledge. As Eric walked towards the exit of what had been his home for the last couple of months, he heard Ekchuah's voice one last time.

"Watch yourself out there, kid."

Eric turned to see his mentor wearing a look of genuine concern. He was reminded that for all his abrasiveness, Ekchuah really was looking out for him.

"Thanks, coach."

With that, Eric walked along the walkway and took his first steps on the terrestrial ground. He saw the doors close on Draco Azul's cockpit as the mech immediately sank back into the ocean. He turned around to see a natural path that led towards a small collection of buildings.

That's where the geyser must be, thought Eric.

The young man then began his trek towards civilization.

***

For the next hour, Eric walked inland until he had reached the main road most people took to get to La Bufadora. Along the way, he kept himself hydrated with his supply of vitamin-infused water. Normally, such a hike would leave him dead tired. While he was never in bad shape, the young man never had much endurance to begin with. Yet he noticed that he never got tired as he trekked along. Perhaps, he thought, this was due to his constant training with Ekchuah.

Through the DraCom, he learned that he had started his journey in Arbolitos Cove. All he had to do was press on the left "eye" on the device and out popped a holographic map showcasing his location, like that of a smartphone app. Once he found out what direction he needed to go in, the rest was easy.

By the time Eric reached the main road, he walked in the direction of the geyser. He watched a few cars pass by him until a black pickup truck stopped just ahead of him. Part of the young man grew nervous, thinking he was about to get mugged, so he slowed down his pace as he was approaching the vehicle. Eric then noticed there were multiple people in the car all talking at once in Spanish. The driver opened the door and out stepped a man who appeared to be in his mid-30s. He wore very casual clothing and did not seem to be wielding any weapons.

"Good afternoon, mister!" the man said in Spanish with a smile.

"Are you heading to La Bufadora?"

Eric remained cautious as he prepared his answer. *"Yes."*

Eric never practiced his Spanish a whole lot, so he kept his answer brief and simple. Despite living in a Mexican American community and being Mexican himself, he never practiced Spanish at all as it was never a necessity where he lived.

"Are you ok, mister?" the stranger asked, puzzled at Eric's nervous behavior. Then his eyes lit up. *"Ah! Forgive me. My name is Ernesto Rodriguez. My family and I were driving down from Tijuana to see the geyser. We wanted to offer you a ride if you were going there."*

Eric slowly began to relax; at the moment it did not seem like these people were a threat.

"I-I am Eric. Eric Martinez. Yes. I am going to La Bufadora."

The white-washed Mexican realized how awkward he must have sounded to Ernesto. With his limited grade-school Spanish, he probably came off as some kind of caveman that just learned how to speak for the first time. His thick American accent did not help matters either.

"Are you from America, mister?" Ernesto asked, in English this time upon hearing his Spanish.

"Yeah… I'm just visiting." Eric continued to lower his defenses.

"Is that so? Well, do you want to ride with us? It's only my wife and kid."

"S-sure. I'd appreciate it," Eric hesitantly replied.

"¡Vamos, pues!" The man said in a joyful manner.

Ernesto opened the door to the back seat and allowed Eric into his truck. There he saw his wife, similar in age to him, and their son who may have been around ten years old. His family all looked at him with smiles.

"Everyone," Ernesto announced to his family in Spanish, *"this here is Eric. He's from America and doesn't speak much Spanish. Now's a good opportunity to practice your English. Especially you, son."*

He then turned to Eric, who was now sitting next to his son. "Eric, this is my family, Julia, and Gustavo."

"H-hey," he said as he awkwardly greeted the pair.

As they began driving, the wife was the first to speak to him.

"Where are you from, Eric?"

"LA. I-I was here on vacation."

"Where exactly?" Ernesto asked.

Eric hesitated as he tried to think of a plausible vacationing spot in Baja California.

"Cabo San Lucas."

The whole family gasped in shock.

"Ay, Dios mio, did you walk the whole way here?" Julia asked.

"Y-yeah, I've been traveling up north since the Diablos started attacking," Eric replied. "I wanted to take a break and see the geyser while I was here."

"I hope you're not planning on crossing the border, *muchacho,"* Ernesto responded.

"Why's that?" the puzzled young man asked.

"It's getting crazy near the border," Julia tried to explain. "Everyone is trying to escape into the US. 'Seeking asylum' is what they call it. But there are so many people that it's taking forever for the US to organize and sort through everyone. In the meantime, the border's been shut down until this whole thing is over."

"Even if you're an American, you'll probably get lost in the shuffle," Julia's husband followed up.

"Well, I lost my passport back at the hotel I stayed at," Eric noted with a chuckle, "so, I guess I'm screwed either way."

He then thought about all the countless lives desperately trying to escape this mess the Diablos started. For whatever reason, these monsters were only appearing in Mexico, mainly inland. Through the reports Ekchuah picked up he learned that everyone down south attempted to evacuate into Central and South America. However, the evacuation had slowed due to the local governments being unable to accommodate so many refugees. It seemed that it did not matter where you lived in Mexico, there was no escape.

"You don't have to worry about the Diablos. Draco Azul will protect us!" proclaimed Gustavo.

"Ah, yes, *mijo,*" Ernesto said in confidence. "God bless that robot. He's made all of us feel safer. In the meantime, we'll be in Ensenada until things calm down in Tijuana."

"Si, mi amor," Julia concurred. "I wish we could talk to whoever's inside Draco Azul. I'd like to know where he came from."

"I still think he's a secret agent in charge of a superweapon built by the world's governments!" the husband postulated.

Eric raised an eyebrow, "What makes you think there's someone piloting Draco Azul?"

"You're right, he could be just a robot," Julia responded. "But don't all big robots have someone inside, driving them like a car?"

"Yeah, like in anime," said Gustavo. "But it doesn't matter, Draco Azul is cool!" the little boy added. "Have you seen it in person, Eric?"

"Don't be silly, *mijo,*" laughed Julia. "Draco Azul hasn't appeared in Baja California. Let's pray that he never has to."

"But what about his bracelet?" the boy inquired. "It looks just like the robot."

Eric panicked as he suddenly realized that he made no attempt to hide his DraCom.

"Uh, it's something I bought back in Cabo," he lied. "I found someone who made it, inspired by the robot. I thought it looked cool and got it."

Disappointment came crashing down on the young child's hopes and dreams. "Oh… well, I really want to see Draco Azul one day."

A smile formed on Eric's face. He had heard of the praise Draco Azul received as a result of his actions, but this was his first time hearing it in person. It was especially surreal hearing other's use the name "Draco Azul," which originally started as Ekchuah's translation of the mech's original Mayan name. Eric stuck with this Spanish translation out of respect for the land he was protecting.

Then something bizarre happened. The public invented that exact same name in the media. Ekchuah informed him that the mech's original name was also invented by the people it once watched over. In his mentor's opinion, it was only fitting that generations later, their descendants would give it the same moniker of "blue dragon." *Life truly is full of surprises*, Eric thought at the time.

"Don't worry, Gustavo," Eric said as he cheered up the boy. "If I ever see Draco or his pilot, I'll tell him you said 'hi.'"

***

Once they arrived at the parking lot near La Bufadora, Eric and the family of three began walking towards the natural landmark. As they strolled by the marketplace, he was disappointed to see that most of the shops had closed as they neared the geyser.

Eric remembered how each tourist location he visited in Mexico was teeming with lively vendors selling all kinds of souvenirs to travelers. He recalled the sight of Mexican candy, pan dulce, handmade glass figurines, Oaxacan wood carvings, absurdly large yet extremely warm blankets, traditional Mexican garbs, piggy banks, and especially t-shirts of copyrighted characters the vendors most certainly did not own. He was never sure why so many of them were of animated characters dressed as gangsters.

As they drew closer towards their destination, Eric could have sworn he saw a shirt bearing a likeness to Draco Azul, but he quickly forgot about it as the group discovered a few restaurants that were open as well, teeming with other tourists. Before Eric tried to explain that he did not have enough money, the kindly father generously offered to pay for his meal.

"You've been through enough. Let us pay for you."

As they sat, they ordered *carne asada* and *adobada* tacos. Eric almost burst into tears as he tasted the juicy and tender beef and marinated pork. It was here that the four of them asked the restaurant's owner why there were still so many tourists, yet so few businesses open. He explained that with so much danger in the country, numerous people have tried to see as much of their beautiful land as they can, in the event that they do not make it. In the case of the vendors at La Bufadora, they essentially had the same idea. Why visit a landmark you practically work at every day?

Eventually, they reached their destination, the great geyser La Bufadora. Dozens of people waited in anticipation of the next periodic burst of water. Saltwater emerged from the cracks of the rocky shore and soared thirty meters into the air. The wind blew the water towards the crowd with everyone gleefully shrieking as they got soaked. It was like watching nature's equivalent of a firework, a very large yet brief explosion to dazzle the crowds if only for a few seconds. Yet, it was those precious seconds that brought a sense of joy strong enough to distract everyone from their harsh reality. Regardless of how short the sensation was, escapism proved to be especially valuable in these trying times.

Eric most definitely enjoyed hearing the sounds of laughter. These were things he had not experienced in quite some time. Though, much like the eruptions of La Bufadora, deep down inside he knew this too was not to last. He had to get back to Draco Azul eventually. Yet, part of him wanted to stay and protect the family that had graciously treated him as one of their own. Who was to say that Ernesto and his family would survive in such a rough climate? He could not leave them and disappear from their lives just like that.

Then he thought about Ekchuah. What would he think if Eric abandoned his responsibilities? Would he be able to find a new pilot to take over? How would the process even work? Such conflicting feelings plagued his mind as he and the Rodriguezes began walking towards the parking lot 45 minutes later.

Suddenly, Eric and company felt the tremors of what seemed like a small earthquake.

"What the hell?" exclaimed Eric as the rest of the people around him responded in a similar manner.

As the tremors subsided, Eric prayed to God that whatever caused the quake wasn't what he thought it could be. He looked over to the Rodriguez family and saw Gustavo embraced in his mother's arms as Ernesto held onto his family. Eric's heart rate increased and his hands were trembling. If this truly was another Diablo attack, it would be the first time he would be in the middle of an attack since he first discovered Draco Azul in Cancun.

The tremors returned, this time even more furious. At that moment, the water levels surrounding La Bufadora began to rise at an alarming rate. Water spilled over into the area where the crowds stood before they all began evacuating.

The DraCom's eyes began flashing yellow. He knew it must be Ekchuah trying to contact him. Eric's worst fears were confirmed. It was a Diablo. He overheard Ernesto getting his family into the car and began calling out to him.

Before he could respond the water levels rose even further, though it wasn't the entire ocean this time -- it was a gargantuan mound rising over the hills themselves. La Bufadora blew one final burst of water into the sky, higher than it ever had before in front of the rising mountain. The presence of this mysterious object must have increased the pressure building inside the sea caves deep beneath the geyser.

The saltwater fell from its amazing heights, revealing to everyone the beast responsible for the great disturbance. Its eyes were as black and soulless as that of a great white shark. Beneath them were two pairs of mandibles like those of a bobbit worm. Draped over its scaly sea-green chest were two enormous manta ray-like fins. It raised its head back and bellowed a terrible screech, its pitch high enough to shatter every piece of glass in the vicinity.

Two thoughts raced through Eric's mind: either escort the Rodriguezes to safety or confront the Diablo head-on. He did not want to abandon them, but at the same time, he would be putting all of Ensenada at risk. Once he made his decision, he rushed over to Ernesto.

"I'm sorry, Ernesto, but you're gonna have to go on without me!"

"What, are you crazy?" the older gentlemen replied. "That Diablo's gonna kill everyone here!"

"I know, that's why I can't go. I gotta-" Eric paused, once more trying to think of another lie; but what he said was no lie at all.

"I gotta make sure everyone else here is safe. If I don't do something, more people are gonna die. Take your family and go!"

The Diablo started taking its first steps out of the water, revealing two feet, each adorned with two claws. It was marching in the direction of the city.

Ernesto was absolutely confused. Then he noticed the flashing watch on Eric's arm. While he could not fully make sense of what Eric was about to do, he understood when a man had made his decision.

"Hold on, *amigo."* Ernesto turned to his car and dug through his luggage. He pulled out a large trench coat and gave it to Eric.

"Take it, it's all I can give you. It's old, but you can sell it for a good amount of money. Do what you can with it."

Eric looked at the coat in his hands and quickly put it on. He reached his hand out to shake Ernesto's hand, but instead, the father embraced him like he was part of the family.

"Que Dios te bendiga, y te lleve con bien," whispered Ernesto before returning to his car.

As the truck started to leave, the young hero noticed Julia and Gustavo shouting at Ernesto to bring Eric along. Both of them stared at Eric as the truck drove off.

With the Rodriguez family out of sight, Eric turned back to the coast. He ran over to the location of the shops to see if anyone had been left behind. There he saw a young man struggling to carry what looked like his grandmother. Within minutes he helped them to their car. In that time, the Diablo was on its way towards the beach town of La Joya.

Eric raised the DraCom to his mouth and loudly recited the first words that came to mind.

"Draco Azul, rise!"

The blinking eyes on the device glowed brighter than ever before. The area started to rumble. The sea levels rose again and once more flooded the exhibition hall, though this time Eric was the only one there. The water rose to his feet, but he did not care.

La Bufadora shot another extremely powerful explosion of water just as it did when the Diablo appeared. This signaled the appearance of Mexico's champion. Up from the depths appeared the metal guardian. The water cascaded off its glistening armor and fell onto Eric, yet his newly acquired coat kept him warm.

Once the giant fully stood, it lowered its hand before Eric. The pilot stepped aboard the mech's appendage, at which point it raised him to its chest, opening before him.

Eric entered the cockpit with Ekchuah there to greet him the only way he knew how.

"Not a bad choice for the command, kid. Though I tried calling you as soon as the Diablo showed up. What were you doing all that time?"

"I was busy. There were people all around and I couldn't exactly reveal myself!" Eric answered as he began to remove his casual wear in preparation for the battle ahead.

"Well, you're lucky you happened to be exactly where the monster showed up."

"Yeah, a bit too lucky. Any idea where it came from?"

"While I was waiting for you to respond, I found a few articles of missing fishing boats along the coast of Baja California. Maybe this thing was submerged in the water for a while until it decided to make its grand debut."

Eric paused at this revelation. By now the nanotech pilot suit was forming itself around his body. At the same time, mechanical arms lowered from the ceiling in order to attach the helmet and limb attachments that calibrated his body's movements to Draco Azul's.

"You think... that thing followed us here?"

"Maybe. Perhaps it was laying low around the coast until it detected us on our way here. The thing must've lost us before settling on attacking Ensenada."

"Oh, god!" Eric fell to his knees at the thought that his selfish actions may have brought more death and destruction to everyone in the city.

Ekchuah was quick to console his student. "Hey! There's no way we could've detected the Diablo, okay? We've never encountered this kind of behavior before. But that's not important right now. What's done is done. Our job now is to go over there and knock its block off!"

Eric stood up and looked over at the trench coat laying on the floor nearby. Ekchuah was right. What he needed to do now was to make sure this monster never hurts anyone ever again.

Eric stretched out his arms, which allowed the chest armor to attach itself to his body, followed by his arms and legs. Finally, the visor-like helmet clung onto Eric's head and from that point on, Draco Azul's body became his own. He could see La Bufadora and its once great bursts of ocean as nothing more than a splash of water to him. He looked into the distance and through Draco's magnifying lenses he could see the Diablo approaching Ensenada, with the Navy attempting to hold it back. He then engaged his mech's wings, rose into the air, and flew in the direction of his enemy.

Within seconds Draco Azul reached the location of the Diablo, having already ravaged through La Joya and El Bajio, and landed right in front of it on the outskirts of the main city. The creature screeched in excitement as if it had seemingly found what it was looking for all this time. The Diablo spread its fins out, revealing four pairs of crustacean limbs, each adorned with thin claws. The devilish sea monster slammed its tail onto the ground as it prepared to attack. The military had held back its assault on the creature as they anticipated both titans' next moves.

"Remember kid, stay on the defense, for now. We don't know what it's capable of." Ekchuah quickly advised his pupil. Eric did not say anything, as his only concern was to keep this fiend away from the city.

The Diablo rushed towards the mech as it braced for impact. Draco Azul raised its arms, blades forward, and blocked the assault from the creature's pincers. The massive size of the beast was able to push the machine back as the blades were incapable of cutting through its thick exoskeleton.

As the leviathan prepared its duel jaws, Eric countered with his crimson scarf. The indestructible cloth wrapped around its target's head. This distracted the beast long enough for Eric to have his robot grab two of the monster's limbs in order to toss it into the ground.

However, Eric had forgotten about the brute's large fins as one of them swiped Draco Azul to the side. The mechanical soldier landed with a shattering thud before being dragged head-first towards its enemy. The Diablo was using the warrior's scarf to bring its prey to it as it was still unable to see. The creature was clearly smarter than it looked.

Eric had his scarf let go of the devil's face and entrap all of its arms. The beast attempted to free itself by latching its jaws onto the scarf, though this act proved futile as Draco Azul used its powerful strength to heave the beast. The Diablo stumbled over its feet and landed on the ground. Eric then retracted his trusty cloth.

While the beast was down, Draco Azul jumped into the air and struck the behemoth's back with enough strength to pierce its armored skin. To Eric and Ekchuah's dismay, the attack drew no blood as its hide proved to be much thicker than they previously thought. Instead, the titanic creature's back started glowing red. Draco Azul backed away from its foe with its pilot unsure of what was about to happen.

The animal got back up on its feet. The red pulsating light then traveled down its body and suddenly shot out from its tail right at the blue giant. Eric felt an enormous pain in his right shoulder as he reeled back from the attack.

"Argh! What the hell was that?"

Ekchuah brought up a holographic screen to rewatch the events they had witnessed moments ago.

"It looks like the creature is able to absorb kinetic energy and convert it into a projectile attack. An ability like this is extremely rare. Heads up!"

Another stream of the Diablo's kinetic blast was shot at Draco Azul's chest before the demon started wildly firing in all directions. Several nearby buildings and neighborhoods were obliterated by the scarlet beams, while some blasts were shot into the distance with impacts too small to be seen.

Eric had his mech duck into the ground while struggling to move his right arm. Ekchuah quickly assessed the damage.

"Don't move it so much, kid. You have a few fractures in your *humerus* and ribs."

"What should we do then?"

"We have to use the Draco Striker, but you have to be careful. An attack like that could cause more trouble for everyone in the vicinity."

Ekchuah had a point, Eric thought. As powerful as Draco Azul's finisher was, it should only be used as a final resort. Depending on the angle of the blast, the surge of lightning would cause untold amounts of damage to the surrounding area. Not to mention how much of a toll the attack will take on Draco Azul as it would sacrifice a hefty amount of the mech's energy reserves. If Eric was going to use it, he had to play it smart.

He noticed that the monster was discharging numerous shots in a frantic manner. It wasn't even trying to aim at him. Why was that? thought Eric. Could it be that the beast was unable to keep all that energy in its body for long and had to expel it quickly? By the time the sadistic Diablo finished expending the last of its fading energy, it turned its sights onto Draco Azul.

"Now's your chance!"

Eric rushed into battle once more, this time using his scarf to hold both his and Draco Azul's right arm in place to avoid further injury. The beast charged as well. However, rather than attacking the metallic figure, the Diablo turned around to absorb the impact. Draco Azul slammed shoulder-first into the creature, but not before stepping on its tail.

"Why'd ya do that? It's gonna fire off another kinetic blast!" Ekchuah exclaimed.

"No, it's not!" shouted Eric before thrusting his remaining left arm down into the Diablo's tail, slicing it off completely in the process.

The hero then summoned as much fury as he could muster into his remaining arm and proceeded to pummel his foe to the ground. The hellspawn attempted to swipe at Draco Azul with its massive fins and claws. Luckily, the pilot reacted quickly enough to roll out of the way. The beast screamed in agony as its back started to glow red again.

With no tail to disperse its built-up energy, however, it began to force itself out from all around its body. Cracks began to form around the giant's chest and blood spurted along its spine. Eric swiftly positioned himself in front of both the savage beast and the ocean in the distance and began charging a concentrated amount of energy into his mech's horn. As the pilot did this, he quickly called out to Ekchuah.

"How much energy is enough to push it into the ocean?"

The look of sudden realization formed on Ekchuah's hologram face, followed by a huge grin.

"Fifty percent should do the trick. Let 'im have it!"

Surges of lightning bolts formed around Draco Azul's horn as the attack built up. Ignoring the intense pain in his chest, Eric took a deep breath before loudly reciting the command needed to unleash his final attack.

"Dracooooo… Strikeeeeeeeeeer!"

On command, the sapphire defender unleashed an intense stream of concentrated lightning at the Diablo. The agonized animal looked toward the beam and before it had the chance to respond, it was caught in the path of the barrage. The demon's feet were lifted off the ground as its body was pushed further and further away from the city and closer towards the beach. Its appendages began to dissolve as did its mandibles. Its body was now burning red hot with its uncontrollable kinetic energy.

Once the blast dissipated, the monster was above the ocean. Before its body fell into the waters, it let out one last defiant screech before it disappeared into the depths below. Shortly thereafter a massive explosion erupted out of the sea as a mass of kinetic energy shot into the sky before eventually dissolving. The battle was over.

***

Several hours later Eric and Ekchuah had parked their giant robot back in Arbolitos Cove. There they reviewed the footage from the local news programs as well as the footage captured by Draco Azul's external cameras. While the Diablos in the past had always attacked Draco Azul whenever it showed up to fight them, this was the first time where one was actively pursuing them. On top of that, this was the first time a Diablo appeared in the sea as opposed to dry land, as if it were waiting all this time to cross paths with their blue bot.

This raised some serious questions on top of the mysterious origins of these monsters. What exactly was driving these beasts and why were they out to destroy Draco Azul specifically? Ekchuah theorized that this may be an extraterrestrial invasion as these creatures continued to display extraordinary abilities and bizarre anatomy not seen on Earth. Though it did not explain how the Diablos kept appearing from beneath the Earth's crust.

Ekchuah also suggested that whoever was pulling the strings may view Draco Azul as enemy number one. Though for that to be possible, they would have to know about the existence of the metal warrior in the first place, despite the robot not appearing in over 800 years. However, such questions would have to be answered at another time as Eric caught something on the news he wished he had never seen.

On the hologram-projected screen, the news displayed the aftermath of the battle across all of Ensenada. Among these reports, Eric caught sight of something familiar. It was revealed that several of the Diablo's kinetic bombardments had fallen on not only El Bajio, but Maneadero as well. From there Eric witnessed a brief glimpse of a totaled black pickup truck with three bodies all covered in white sheets next to it as a result of a massive crater nearby.

"Stop that clip!" shouted a hysterical Eric.

"Found something, kid?"

"I said stop the clip! Zoom in." Eric was now sweating bullets.

In his mind, the word "no" kept repeating over and over again, racing between dread and panic. Ekchuah was surprised to see his protégé in such a disturbed state.

Once Eric got a closer look at the scene, he was able to confirm the ultimate fate of the Rodriguez family. Suddenly, all of his "no's" had changed to "why's." *Why did this have to happen to them? They were safe. They should've been safe. They were nowhere near the fight. Why did this have to happen to them? Why them? Why them!*

Then as the grief-stricken pilot collapsed on his knees did he begin to feel hatred towards himself. Had he been more careful, the Diablo would not have shot out that blast at them. Had he not accepted their help, they would have left La Budadora earlier. Had he not come to Ensenada at all, they would have been alive. Everyone would have been alive if it were not for his selfish need for a damn break. Maybe that monster would have remained sleeping at the bottom of the ocean forever.

Tears streamed down the young man's face as he mourned his loss. Ekchuah could tell that Eric was distraught, as he had seen enough pilots go through the same torturous ordeal. For his past pupils, they each had friends and families to console them through the toughest of times. Unfortunately for Eric, he had none. Ekchuah gently placed his hand on his student's shoulder and did the best he could to comfort his friend and ally.

"Kid… Eric, I'm truly sorry. They must've meant a lot to you, and it's awful. If you're blaming yourself, don't. You did your best to save as many lives as you can, though you're never gonna save them all. It's one of the harshest lessons every pilot goes through. But what lives you did save will live on because of you. And that's what we need to do, protect those we can save and preserve the memories of those we've lost."

Eric looked up at Ekchuah, feeling no less sad for Ernesto, Julia, and little Gustavo. He had always known of the casualties from past battles, but this was the first time where he truly experienced pain for the people he towered over.

The pilot then stared over at the trench coat beside him. He picked it up and draped it over himself like a blanket. He learned what it meant to fail at his duty and promised never to let it happen to anyone ever again. He would continue training and improving his skills as a pilot and fight to the bitter end. He would not stay in one location waiting for danger to come out of hiding. Rather, he would use Draco Azul to travel the land until he hunts down every damn Diablo he could find.

However, with such dedication to his cause, his isolation would continue to grow as he feared bringing anyone else into his violent world will only cause more pain and misery. Grief has the capability to strengthen a person as much as it can destroy them. Whether or not one becomes consumed by one's own sorrow is ultimately in each individual's hands. How will this grief affect poor Eric Martinez? He would have to find out for himself on the field of battle, for that was the path he had chosen.

END

DRACO AZUL: A FRIEND FROM AFAR

In the dark, busy streets of Playa del Carmen, a man ran in pursuit of his target. The suspect had the appearance of an adult male in his early thirties, dressed head to toe in designer clothing, and decorated in jewelry. He would look like an ordinary man who went for a night out on the town if it were not for his blood-stained hands. The only thing more suspicious than his hands was his pursuer's wardrobe. He looked like something out of an old spaghetti western with his poncho draped over a leather vest and buttoned-up shirt. The pursuer ran on sturdy boots while holding on to his ten-gallon hat. Hanging from his belt were two holsters with each holding silver revolvers.

As the pursuer and pursued played their game of cat and mouse through the nightlife of Mexico's fastest-growing coastal town, the target attempted to lose the hunter within the massive crowds of bar and club-goers. The well-dressed dandy fit right among the young impressionable men and women, who simply wanted to escape their worries and temporarily forget about the ongoings that have plagued their country. The cowboy, on the other hand, stood out from every crowd in the vicinity.

The dandy shoved aside anyone who was in his way, all while the cowboy did his best not to bring harm to any of the pedestrians. The fleeting runaway quickly turned around the corner of a particular night club.

The hunter followed suit, only to find that his prey was nowhere to be seen. The cowboy slowly removed one of his revolvers from his belt and cautiously walked along the narrow passage. The club's neon lights shined through the windows and reflected on his gun. The hunter came to a standstill as the alley split into several paths, each devoid of light. Left with no option, the man crouched down and leaped five stories into the air. While airborne, he inspected all three pathways until he landed atop one of the buildings.

The moment the cowboy's feet touched the roof of the building he was struck from behind and was knocked off the edifice. The man crashed into one of the alleys, sustaining even further injuries. He struggled to get up until he felt the pressure of a foot forcing him down. However, this was no normal foot... he could feel a single-hoofed limb piercing into his back, all while hearing a deep laugh.

The hunter had become the hunted and would have been dead had it not been for a pair of police officers making arrests just outside the club. The cowboy felt the abnormal foot's weight lift, allowing him to see what appeared to be a distorted form of the dandy running ahead of him, disappearing into the darkness. Desperate, the cowboy aimed his gun. The revolver began to glimmer a dim white light. With no strength left, the light faded away as he began to lose consciousness, his target escaping. Before passing out, a random newspaper flew into his face. The last image he saw was a headline article, one of a larger-than-life savior for a country in peril.

One week later…

Danger had fallen on Durango City as man and machine engaged in a fight to the death. Fighting on behalf of Mexico and the entire world was the mechanical giant robot, Draco Azul. Opposite to the azure knight was the latest in a long line of mysterious nightmares that have plagued Mexico for months, a Diablo. While Draco Azul had fought off numerous Diablos of various forms, this one was unlike anything the human race had ever encountered.

It was clearly plant-like, yet its overall form was like that of an animal, a body with a head and six limbs. It growled and moved its body like that of a leopard as it clawed at the heavily armored exterior of the mech. However, for Draco Azul's pilot, Eric Martinez, and his AI companion and mentor, Ekchuah, they would not let this monster lay harm to Mexico any longer.

Ever since the incident in Ensenada, Eric and Ekchuah have been traveling the land, never staying in one location for too long, in pursuit of the Diablos that may be hiding around the country. Through their access to all the latest news, they discovered reports of dwindling vegetation within the arid region of central Mexico, which brought them to Durango City.

Once the pair arrived, they discovered the source of the dying plant life, a massive parasitic creature that had been growing just outside the city within the larger Guadiana Valley. Upon discovery, the creature had removed itself from the ground, revealing its bestial form and attacked Draco Azul.

Their fight eventually brought them into the city. There the creature used its thorn-riddled vines to absorb the nutrients from the surrounding vegetation to heal itself from the wounds inflicted by Draco Azul's blades.

Now fully recovered, the botanical beast unleashed a flurry of vines from its back to incapacitate the mech to where not even its weapons were enough to defend itself. Inside the mech's cockpit, Eric and Ekchuah struggled to plan their next move.

"How are the Draco Wings? Can we fly ourselves outta here?" the pilot asked.

"No can do, kid. The vines are getting in the way," replied the holographic form of Ekchuah as he inspected Draco Azul's specs through a series of screens he brought up. "Our only option is the Draco Striker. The power's more than enough to sear these vines and burn that damn weed to a crisp!"

"Why couldn't we have done that to begin with?" Eric seethed.

"I keep telling ya, all lightning-based attacks should only be used as a last resort! Not only are they dangerous, but they also take a lot of juice."

"Alright, alright! Here goes nothing."

But just as he was about to recite the vocal command, a streak of light zipped by his line of sight. In that instance, the vines that had once restricted his arms were swiftly free.

The Diablo roared in confusion and pulled back its remaining vines.

"What the heck was that?" he asked bewilderedly.

"No idea, but it looks like the Diablo's retreating. Get 'im now while it's confused!" advised Ekchuah.

Eric leaped into action by having Draco Azul grab onto its crimson red scarf and lasso the monster's vines. The creature resisted and attempted to break free, but its strength was no match for the robot's otherworldly might. With one mighty tug, Draco Azul pulled the Diablo towards it where it proceeded to pummel the behemoth until its body fell limp as green juices oozed out from its corpse.

Once Eric regained his composure, he studied the area to find the source of the light.

"I knew it shot upwards from the ground," Eric said to himself as he scanned the now evacuated streets of Durango City.

That was when he noticed a bizarre-looking human, standing all alone, smirking at him.

"Uh, coach? You see what I'm seeing?"

"The cowboy? Yeah, I didn't know those guys were still around."

"Not really, outside of movies and ranches... I think." Eric was unsure of what to make of the man.

Just then, the killer plant jumped at Draco Azul and knocked it to the ground near the cowboy. Its vines lashed everywhere, scraping the robot's armor and ripping apart the ground around the cowboy.

Eric, using his mech's arm, attempted to shield the odd man from the vines, all while keeping the Diablo from biting at his face.

"Dammit, what's with this guy? Why isn't he running away?"

Eric was ready to lose it when suddenly he saw the cowboy jumping onto Draco Azul's arm with implausible strength.

"What the-!" both Eric and Ekchuah were left gasping as the cowboy took out a gun and shot a blast of bright energy aimed squarely at the plant monster's cranium.

The explosive impact was enough to blow off a chunk of its head, driving the beast back. Eric looked back at his arm, only to see that the cowboy was nowhere in sight.

Once more the creature dug its vines into the ground in a vain attempt to heal itself. Seeing a perfect opportunity, Eric went in for the kill.

"Draco Strikeeeeer!"

A small, concentrated beam of lightning surged from the horn on Draco Azul's forehead and incinerated the Diablo's head. Its body fell limp as it was engulfed in flames.

"Glad that's over, but I think we could've finished it off without resorting to the Draco Striker, kid... kid?" Ekchuah called out to his student multiple times, but the pilot was too focused at the spot where the strange super cowboy once stood.

"What was he?" Eric whispered under his breath.

"Eric!"

"Huh, what?"

"I don't know who that guy was, but we can't lollygag around here."

Ekchuah was right, with the Diablo gone the local authorities and civilians were going to crowd the streets in a few moments to witness the aftermath of the battle. Both Eric and Ekchuah agreed that the giant robot was far too dangerous to be around people. On top of that, law enforcement and the Army were nowhere near the point of seeing the mech as anything other than another threat. Eric activated the metal goliath's wings and launched into the valley.

Meanwhile, men and women began surrounding the burning corpse of the fallen Diablo. Unbeknownst to everyone, a single vine had long since detached itself in a desperate attempt to flee its fiery fate. After managing to slither away before the crowds gathered *en masse,* the botanical tendril slipped away into the sewers below the city.

***

After escaping deep into Guadiana Valley, a massive region within the larger state of Durango, Eric and Ekchuah had Draco Azul hidden between a set of hills, hidden from any prying eyes. Within the seated robot, the two reviewed the footage of their recent fight within the cockpit of the azure knight. The pair played back footage of their mysterious accomplice, repeatedly seeing if they could decipher the stranger's identity.

Upon zooming in and digitally recreating the image, Ekchuah managed to make out the finer details of the man. He was of average height, had a light brown complexion, dark black hair, and wore a thick mustache. Clothing wise, he dressed head to toe in an outfit that made him fit right at home in a Clint Eastwood flick, especially the massive hat and poncho that covered most of his body.

"Beyond his fashion sense, he looks like a normal human," explained Ekchuah.

"You're kidding? The guy jumped over Draco like it was nothing," Eric responded. "Plus, there's that weird gun he used. Could we get a better look at it?"

Ekchuah answered by playing the footage to the point where the man took out his gun. The AI then enhanced the image to better focus on the weapon.

The device had the overall shape of a revolver, except it featured a more angular aesthetic, unlike anything Eric had seen. The gun also had an oddly bright color scheme, featuring a silver frame & barrel and a navy-blue handle with a gold star-shaped insignia. The most puzzling aspect of the design was that it featured no traditional chamber where a normal gun's bullets are kept. Though given what it was able to do to the Diablo, whatever bullets it used certainly did not need any regular storage compartment.

Ekchuah pulled up numerous reference images of every revolver model he could find on the Internet, his source for all the ongoings in the world, especially when it came to Diablo activity. However, Ekchuah only grew more frustrated with each failed match.

"Nothing! Whatever it is, it probably isn't even from Earth."

"Why… don't we try asking him ourselves?" Eric said, unsure of his own words.

"Hmph. Right. Like Mr. Desperado here is gonna show up at our doorstep."

"Well, what if I told you he just did so?"

"What are you going on about?"

Ekchuah turned to look at his pupil, only to see him facing the front screen of the cockpit that displayed Draco Azul's vision. Indeed, right before their eyes stood the bizarre cowboy, standing before the robot with the cheekiest grin they had ever seen.

The lone gunman waved at the robot, hoping for an answer.

"Damn, how'd he find us!" Eric panicked.

"More importantly, what does he want with Draco?" queried Ekchuah.

Eric peered closely at the lone figure and noticed his mouth was moving.

"It looks like he's speaking to us."

With a wave of his hand, Ekchuah activated the speakers within the cockpit. In that instance, the upbeat voice of the stranger filled the room.

"*Excuse me? Hello? I'm sorry to bother you, but I must speak with the pilot inside.*" The cowboy was using Spanish, and his formality took Eric by surprise for a person who dressed so rugged.

"Or, perhaps you speak English? I understand it's the most popular language on your planet." The stranger caught the pilot off guard as he spoke his language as perfectly as he did with Spanish.

Hold on, Eric thought, *what did he just say?*

"'Your planet?' Could he… no, it can't be." Eric second-guessed himself.

"You're saying an alien disguised as a human is impossible, yet a sixty-meter robot from space isn't?" the holographic entity pointed out.

55

"I beg you, the fate of this world, and others out there depend on us. Time is of the essence!" the man pleaded.

"I'm not detecting any suspicious patterns in his speech. From what I can tell he's speaking the truth," Ekchuah confirmed. "It's up to you, kid."

Eric thought of what to do with this bizarre visitor. If the stranger was sincere, and the world was under a new threat, he knew he couldn't take any chances if lives were on the line. He walked towards the center of the cockpit. The floor glowed as he entered the field in which to pilot his gargantuan machine. His head, once free of technology, became wrapped in the nanomachines that composed his pilot suit, leaving all but his eyes, nose, mouth, and chin exposed.

"Suit me up, coach," Eric requested.

"As you wish, kid." With another wave of his hand, Ekchuah summoned forth multiple appendages from the ceiling to bring forth the rest of Eric's equipment. Each machine attached devices on Eric's chest, back, legs, and arms, and topped it off with a visor that would give him the sight of the Primal Warrior, Draco Azul. Once his suit was activated, Eric assumed the position of his titanic avatar, which sat before the diminutive cowboy.

Once calibrations were set, the robot's vision became his, and Eric could witness the diminutive form of the cowboy who was supposedly from space.

"Who are you," Eric said, with his voice booming through his mech's external speakers. "And what is this threat you speak of?"

"Ah, finally!" the cowboy shouted gleefully. "I knew those last words would pique your interest."

The man leaped hundreds of feet into the air and landed on Draco Azul's shoulder. Eric jumped to his feet alarmed.

"Gah! Don't do that!" Eric noticed the man reeling in pain from his sudden outburst. "Sorry."

"It's alright," said the cowboy as he rubbed his ears, "I've heard far worse throughout my adventures." The man puffed out his chest as he prepared to introduce himself.

"I have been given many names on the numerous planets I have visited. However, the title I chose to bear is 'Star Slinger,' the greatest bounty hunter in the galaxy! Enemy to all ne'er-do-wells across all planets!" The man struck a pose as his left fist rested on his hip and his right thumb pointed at his smiling face. If he was any more exuberant, he'd have explosions erupting behind him.

A bounty hunter… from space? the perplexed pilot thought.

"Hmm, quite the ego on this guy, but I like his enthusiasm," the AI retorted as he gave his approval.

"However, since stationing here on your planet, I've adopted the alias 'José.' Refer to me however you'd like."

"Okay, um… José, what is it you're here for?" Eric asked the bounty hunter.

"For my latest bounty, I've been tasked to track down a notorious killer known as Varukan. He's had a massive record of preying on sentient life, a crime punishable by law, and one I will not allow as long as my heart still beats! For the last month, I've tried tracking him down and our chase led me to this planet. I almost caught him in Playa del Carmen, but he proved too strong and cunning for me to tackle alone. That's where *you* come in!"

Eric was taken aback as he imagined a lumbering Draco Azul chasing around a human-sized extraterrestrial through the streets.

"Hold on, how do you expect me to catch a tiny alien serial killer? I'll only end up causing tons of destruction!"

"Ah, but it's not your robot that I need," the cowboy grinned as he pointed to the mech's chest. "Rather it's *you*, the very pilot inside this wonderful machine! With your help, we can track down Varukan together, and once he's cornered, we can spring our trap with Draco Azul if he decides to grow to his true size."

"His… true… size?" Eric shuttered to think what those words could mean for a deadly murderer from outer space.

"Why yes, species like he and I can shed our disguises and grow to proportions equal to that of your machine. I only appear before you now as a human in the hopes of blending in with your people."

At that moment Ekchuah scoffed at José's remark.

"If that getup is what he calls a disguise then he's probably spent too much time studying the wrong century."

"Either that or he's way too into the whole gunslinger theme," Eric replied.

"I'm sorry, what was that?" questioned the spaceman.

"Oh! N-nothing, I was just thinking out loud!"

Eric then heard his mentor speak up.

"Alright, kid. The way I see it, we have three options. We either look for this Varukan guy ourselves, follow whatever it is the cowboy wants us to do, or we let him do all the work while we stay safe inside Draco. The choice is yours. Just so you know, I'm still not picking up anything suspicious from his speech patterns. However, he could be an excellent liar."

Unsure if he could trust this potential ally, Eric struggled to determine what the best course of action was. Should he risk being exposed, or potentially killed, should he decide to step outside Draco Azul? Would it be best to stay out of the city until the threat literally grows too big for one person to handle? Or, could he go out and face this unknown homicidal foe alone? After thinking it over, he ultimately went with his gut.

"I'll follow you wherever Varukan is and leave Draco on autopilot until we need him."

"Excellent!" José said before being interrupted by Draco Azul's massive hand, now pointing at him with a massive index finger.

"But listen here. If you end up backstabbing me, I'll have Draco Azul chase you down from beyond the grave!"

Eric himself knew Ekchuah was not capable of piloting the mech to such an extent as too much input from both the AI and the entire machine would cause the entire system to crash. The alien race that created the robot specifically designed it to function this way as they wanted the planet's dominant species to be fully responsible for whatever actions it made and not leave it in the hands of an automatic system. As far as Eric knew, José did not know any of this and hoped to God that his bluff would pay off.

The desperado chuckled as if amused by the threat.

"Heh, you certainly needn't worry about me. You have my word. However!" The spaceman pointed his own finger back at the mech. "I'm more concerned about *you*! Your fight with the Rozacdyl left much to be desired."

Rozacdyl? Eric thought to himself. *That thing had a name?*

"Therefore, I need to test you to see if you're ready to take on an average-sized opponent."

As annoyed as he was with his words, Eric realized that the man did have a point. He had never gone up against an enemy outside of his robot, and if he could eliminate the problem before it could escalate to a gargantuan scale, then all the better for the civilians.

Eric immediately disengaged the controls and detached himself from his equipment, leaving only his nanotech suit covering his entire body.

"Open the door, coach," requested the pilot.

"Eric, are you crazy?" Ekchuah protested.

"Maybe, but I need to know for myself how well I can do. Keep Draco ready if something happens."

"Geez. Alright, kid. It's your funeral."

With the door to the outside world unlocked, Eric stepped outside aboard Draco Azul's hand. Upon lowering itself to the ground, with Ekchuah behind the controls, Eric got to see the man that called himself "Star Slinger" face to face. After the two sized each other up, José decided to be the first to speak.

"It's a pleasure to meet the man behind this magnificent piece of machinery." José then shifted his eyes back towards Draco Azul and gazed in awe at its presence.

"Y'know, for years I've heard rumors of an exceptional race that once donated robotic technology to several less advanced planets, but I'd never thought I'd see one for myself."

"I'm flattered," Eric said sarcastically, still suspicious of the overly enthusiastic alien.

"Alright, how do you want to do this?"

"How's this?" the bounty hunter suggested. "The first to land a single hit wins. No weapons, only straightforward hand-to-hand combat."

The man removed his poncho, along with his weapons to prove he was serious. As he laid his items to the ground, Eric caught sight of his two revolvers, along with a strange leather-wrapped rod he took out from a sheath behind his back, attached to his belt.

José raised his hands like a boxer, yet kept his palms open like he was about to karate chop his rival. Eric readied himself as well.

"Fine by me."

The mech pilot immediately went straight for the kill but was astonished by how quickly his opponent reacted to each and every one of his swings. All while shining his Cheshire grin. It seemed he was having fun more than anything.

Eric recalled his simulated sparring sessions with Ekchuah, remembering his lessons in searching for and exploiting his enemies' weaknesses. Yet, the cowboy moved far too fast for him to gain a sense of his fighting style.

Just then, the ranchero leaped into the air with his superhuman strength. Eric looked up at the sky, only to be blinded by the sun's rays. Expecting an attack from above, he raised both arms and felt the force of what felt like a 300-pound sofa crashing down on his limbs. Yet, he did not budge. He gritted his teeth and bore the pain, as he did whenever Draco Azul came across combatants far stronger and heavier.

He could feel it was José's foot on his arms. The poncho-wearing gentleman jumped off Eric's arms, pushing the young man to the ground.

"You may be a bit slow, but you can certainly take a great deal of pain. I won't count that since you blocked it. But I will count this."

José ran towards Eric, still on the ground recovering. With quick thinking, he rolled to the side as his foe threw a punch at the ground, breaking the soil beneath him. The shockwave sent Eric reeling.

His opponent turned his attention back on him just as Eric finally got back on his feet. The young man had never encountered an opponent as strong as José. He realized he had no hope of landing a hit unless, however, he could get close enough.

Again, the cowboy rushed towards his adversary, as did the mech pilot towards his challenger. Both men prepared to throw one last punch towards each other.

José smiled at what he believed was his victory. But something was not right. At the last possible moment, Eric stopped in place, twisted his torso, and thrust his elbow right into his rival's gut.

The force of the impact, combined with the immense strength of his inhuman opponent, not only fractured Eric's elbow but also pushed him ten feet away from José. His entire arm would've been destroyed had it not been for his durable pilot suit. As he writhed in pain, his rival stood in place, still in shock that his opponent managed to get the upper hand.

A smile formed on his face before he noticed the massive robot reaching out to the injured victor.

He ran towards Eric and grabbed onto his broken arm.

"Hold on, big guy!" shouted José as Draco Azul's hand was mere feet away from the duo. "I'll take care of this!"

Eric saw his right arm glow in a bright warm aura of white light. All the pain he was experiencing was gone in an instant. As José let go, Eric moved his arm and found that his injury was completely healed. He called out to Ekchuah.

"It's ok, I'm fine!"

Draco Azul backed off while still keeping its eyes on Eric and José.

"Boy, that's some AI program you have on there," José commented.

"Trust me, you don't know the half of it."

"Oh, I believe you. There's certainly more to you than I initially thought. That goes for your machine as well. Pretty clever of you to have me come to you for that win. Though, it was foolish of you to sacrifice your arm. You're lucky I could heal you."

"Great, now you're sounding like my coach," said Eric as he rolled his eyes in annoyance.

"Who?"

"Forget it. Are we gonna track this Varukan guy or what?"

"Hmph, straight to the point. Fine then, you've proven your worth. So, let us set out to where I believe is the fiend's latest location, the city of Guanajuato!"

***

Walking out of a bar in the middle of the night was 22-year-old Paula Guzmán and her rowdy gaggle of friends. In the weeks since their college shut down in response to the Diablo attacks, Paula and company partied like it was the end of the world every chance they could get. If life was gonna come crashing down on them, why not go out with a bang, she thought.

On this particular night, she and her male and female companions encountered a charismatic individual with a suave demeanor and a lust for excitement equal to hers. The man introduced himself as Balthazar and had convinced the party of five to travel with him to a secret VIP club he was privy to. His devilish charm had convinced the women, who in turn convinced the men to follow their new acquaintance.

While Paula initially wanted to call for a taxi, Balthazar scoffed at the notion, explaining that the joint must be kept secret and that he was only allowed to bring up to five guests in a single year. After walking for what seemed like forever, Paula's buzz began to wear off as she started noticing that they had walked in an unfamiliar part of town. She realized that Balthazar had taken them to a street tunnel.

Paula asked Balthazar how long it would take. His response was a simple "soon enough." She started feeling uncomfortable and noticed that her friends were still riding off their alcohol-infused high.

She tried to convince her friends that it was getting late and it was time for them to go back home. Sadly, the point at which she went against Balthazar's wishes was the moment where she would find herself at the premature end of her journey.

To her disbelief, she witnessed Balthazar's hands growing and distorting in shape. They became two massive pairs of serrated claws. His claws lashed out two elongated tentacles and began eviscerating two of her best friends. She and her remaining companions ran for their lives.

Still inebriated, her remaining male friend tripped and fell. To her horror, he was lassoed by a slimy tentacle and was pulled towards the inhuman killer. As he screamed his life away, she could hear a deep, menacing laugh.

Paula grabbed her last friend's arm only to find her lone partner pierced through the chest by a second harpoon-like tentacle. Realizing that her friends were all goners she ran as fast she could, crying hysterically as she made her escape.

Once more, she heard the low-pitch laugh. Though, it did not come from behind her, nor in front. In fact, it did not seem to come from any direction. Was it all in her head, she thought? The laughing grew louder and louder as it deepened further until it drowned out every sound around her.

Just then, a massive shadow leaped over her and stood in her path on the empty streets of this seemingly abandoned district. The shadow was hidden in the flickering streetlights. It did not look human at all. It was seven feet tall and had pine cone-like growths and hair all over its body. Its legs were contorted like that of a digitigrade animal and sported hooves. She glanced at its horned head as four pairs of glowing red eyes gazed down at her. It raised its pincer-like hands.

There was no doubt that whatever this monstrosity was, it was Balthazar. Paula screamed for her life, but unfortunately for her, all she could hear was the creature's never-ending laugh.

***

It was the following evening, as Eric and José walked around the streets of Guanajuato City. Eric decided to wear his nanotech suit underneath his street clothes for protection. He also kept his DraCom communicator hidden under his long coat. With it, he touched base with Ekchuah, who had hidden Draco Azul near the city.

It was only a few hours ago that Eric and Ekchuah escorted their new ally to Guanajuato, a city famous for its nearly 200-year-old mummies.

Gee, a fittingly grim place for a string of murders, Eric thought on the way there.

Ekchuah, still not trustful of José, had him seated in Draco Azul's hands when they flew towards their destination. While José could have traveled on his own, he explained that doing so would have alerted Varukan.

"Yeah, right," Ekchuah told Eric upon hearing his excuse, "as if a giant robot wasn't any less suspicious."

Yet, miraculously, they managed to make it to the city without any hassles. The only issue Eric had was hearing how much Ekchuah disliked the bounty hunter.

At least I managed to keep him from dropping José, which was all Eric could be thankful for.

Now that the mech pilot and bounty hunter were situated in the downtown portion of the city, the two scoured for any info they could find, be it newspapers, locals, or radio newscasts. Luckily for Eric, José kept a decent chunk of perfectly counterfeited currency to pay off his informants.

"When you're looking for bounties, you always gotta carry a healthy supply of cash," boasted the buckaroo.

From what they had gathered, the recent string of gruesome murders and missing person reports have all involved young men and women within their early to mid-twenties. Occasionally pieces of their corpses were discovered near the many tunnels of the city. Sometimes it was a finger, sometimes it was a foot. Other times it was hair or tiny scraps of clothing. The police have already gotten involved, but due to the daily traffic flow, investigating the tunnels proved difficult.

Also, unless money was involved, no officer wanted to catch themselves becoming the next midnight victim. Such is the life of a corrupt law enforcement system driven by low wages. It also did not help that there was already widespread panic and paranoia over the ongoing Diablo attacks.

"So far, everything is in accordance with his modus operandi," José theorized as he and Eric exchanged notes at a local taqueria.

"You think so?" Eric inquired.

"It's always the same. He enjoys a wealthy night on the town, indulges in all manners of luxury, and caps it off by feasting on a victim or two."

"He seems to have already made quite a stir."

"Right, it's like he's challenging us. Daring me to confront him." The intensity in José's voice grew. "He's definitely up to something!"

***

As the streets grew less crowded, Eric and José began walking towards the tunnels, figuring it was where Varukan was most likely hiding. As they made their way there, Eric decided to find out more about his acquaintance.

"So… what's up with the duds?"

"Pardon?"

"The clothes. Haven't you noticed that you stick out like a sore thumb?"

José inspected his wardrobe, then glanced at the random pedestrians around him.

"Perhaps, but it's the attire I feel speaks to me the most. The same goes for the name."

"How so?"

"During my time on this planet, I found it to be one of the most common names in this region. I thought it'd be perfect for keeping my anonymity in check. I suppose you'd know a thing or two about hiding from the public."

Eric was slightly taken aback by his remark. How would he know about how he operates?

"I could tell from all the stories I hear that you show up when needed, then leave as soon as your work is done. You don't bask in your glory; rather, you go into hiding, waiting for your next battle. I respect that. Like you, I also wish to remain hidden."

Strange he'd say that when he's walking around in a poncho and leather boots, Eric thought.

"I don't know how your people view bounty hunters, but I'm only out for justice. Any criminal that dares to abuse their power over other's lives is simply unacceptable!"

Right on cue, José's grandiose persona rose to the occasion. Meanwhile, Eric covered his face, embarrassed at his colleague's over the top bravado.

"And that's why I knew I could count on you. You've got the spirit of a true hero."

A true hero? Eric contemplated what those words meant. He had grown up watching flashy and courageous characters on both the silver screen and television. As much as Eric entertained himself with the idea of being like them as a child, he had never considered himself a "true hero" like José was suggesting.

In fact, the only reason he kept fighting against the Diablos was that he felt he had no other option. He saw himself being trapped under a moral obligation to save lives after stumbling across Draco Azul deep beneath Cancun on that fateful day. Was this what being a "true hero" really was?

"I don't know if I'd go that far," Eric responded. "I'm only here 'cause I have to be."

"Well, you certainly aren't going to be a true hero if you continue rushing into battles and breaking elbows." José let out a huge laugh, angering Eric in the process.

What's with this guy? was all the young man could think of in response.

***

Eventually, the two of them reached the city's tunnel system. By then, the streets were barren beyond the occasional homeless vagrant. Before the pair entered the tunnels, Eric had the nanotech that composed his suit expand to cover his hands and head. José handed Eric one of his revolvers, but not before it glowed in his hand with the same white illumination he had seen in Durango. The gun felt strangely warm once it was passed to him.

"What did you do to it?" Eric asked.

"These are specialized weapons that feed off my life energy by converting it into ammunition. The more times I use it, the weaker I get. At least until I get a chance to recharge."

"Wow, so you can't afford to waste any bullets."

"Lucky for you, good sir, I don't," said José as he flashed another cheeky grin.

The deeper they entered the vacant passages the more unnerved Eric grew. Already uncomfortable holding a gun for the first time in his life, he was doubting if he could possibly use it even if his life depended on it. The only comforting thought was that his DraCom still worked as its advanced technology allowed its signal to pass through the thick layers of concrete separating him from the outside world. As they dived into the underground levels, they continued to find no clues. That was until José picked up something with his superhuman vision.

"I see traces of blood. Varukan's definitely been through here."

He scanned the entire area and found that the trail of dry blood, only a day old, had stretched out into another part of the tunnels, potentially from another entrance altogether.

Eric held onto his gun tightly and allowed José to take the lead. They were entering a section of the road devoid of streetlights. He could not even see his own hand in front of him. José then raised his gun and illuminated his barrel with a charging blast of energy.

"Won't that give us away?" Eric asked.

"I'm counting on it," whispered José. "Keep a lookout."

José shot a projectile that illuminated the entire passage as it traveled down the wide channel. Another fire was immediately shot from the revolver. This time, the energy bullet was significantly smaller and traveled much faster. Eric caught a glimpse of something moving along the wall about fifty feet away from them.

Acting on impulse, he raised his gun and fired wildly in the general direction. The first two shots missed with the third grazing the creature's arm. Somehow, its painful shrieks blasted within Eric's head. It felt as though he was experiencing a migraine. As he clung onto his cranium, he felt José's hand on his forehead, and the pain immediately subsided.

"My apologies. I should've warned you that he could attack others through low-level telepathy. I was hoping we could get the drop on him before he'd try something like that."

Eric was stunned. José could have easily chased after Varukan, but instead chose to help him. However, there was no time to think about that. At the moment, they had a killer to catch.

Once José recharged Eric's revolver, the two ran down the passage. At a fork in the road, they noticed the stream of fresh blood entering the left passage.

"This might be a diversion. You take the right, I'll go left!"

Without hesitating, Eric followed his advice. As he ran down the enclosed aisle he pressed the trigger on his gun as José had done earlier. He was able to charge a shot while illuminating the hallway. Yet, he realized that the longer he held onto his charge shot, the more ammo it would take up. He decided this would be his one single shot, firing it when the need arose.

He came across a staircase, a shortcut to the surface. Varukan could have easily taken these stairs to escape, but what if this too was another diversion? As Eric hesitated, he found that his revolver had reached peak luminosity. Whatever amount of ammo he had, this was it.

If I'm getting ambushed, it might as well be out in the open.

Eric quickly ran up the stairs and out into the streets above. Once he reached the ground level, he heard the sound of a slithery, slimy object approaching him. He turned to see what it was as an elongated object from the alien's hand slammed into his chest with the force of a brick. While this object tore through his shirt, he was thankful that his nano suit prevented him from becoming a human shish kabob. Understanding that this slimy appendage was connected to the creature, he grabbed onto it and fired his gun.

Witnessing the massive projectile approaching, the extraterrestrial sliced off his tentacle with his other hand to escape. The burst of light blew up a closed shop behind him. The resulting explosion knocked the creature off his feet.

Eric could finally see the murderous fiend clearly. His massive body was covered in fur and armor. His hands were not hands at all, but giant tooth-filled mouths, making the severed appendage his tongue. This frightening being was Varukan.

With no way to contact José, Eric had only one option left. He raised the DraCom to his mouth.

"Draco Azul, *rise!*"

Now he had to last the next couple minutes before Ekchuah could bring the Primal Warrior to his location.

Varukan staggered as he got back up. A low-pitched growl emanated from within Eric's mind. Understanding that it used telepathy, he spoke out loud at the alien.

"What are you doing here, Varukan?"

The growling in his head came to a stop and was slowly replaced by a burst of equally chilling laughter.

I suppose that pretentious bounty hunter told you who I was, spoke the alien. *If so, then you already know what I want: all of life's pleasures... and sustenance.*

"But why Earth, why *here* of all places?" Eric shouted.

Cognizant life is always the most delectable. Oh, how I enjoy their screams as I feast upon their innards. And with the recent appearance of giant beasts within this region, it was the perfect cover for my victims' disappearances!

This much Eric knew, but as long as he could keep this fiendish butcher talking, the longer he could stay alive.

"Yeah? Well, you're not getting away with it any longer!"

Ha! You've clearly been spending too much time with that insufferable bounty hunter. You almost sound like him.

"Of course, I do! He's the greatest bounty hunter after all!"

Eric then assumed José's pose, complete with his thumb pointed at his exaggerated grin. Though, as much as he was smiling, his heart was beating with anxiety.

Enough! Varukan screamed, clearly annoyed at Eric's false boasting. *You're gonna die right here, right now!*

The alien ran towards Eric, mouth hands open. The pilot did his best to avoid his enemy's massive swipes and attempted to land a few blows. His attacks, unfortunately, left very little impact on the villain's hulking figure. Varukan lassoed his remaining tongue around Eric's waist and flung him around, smashing him into the multiple nearby buildings before landing on the ground. The serial killer's remaining hand-mouth opened wide and attempted to clamp down on Eric's head. With all his strength, the young man held out his arms and kept the jaws from closing in on his skull. Once more, his suit kept Varukan from slicing through his flesh. All the while the alien laughed maniacally as his prey's strength depleted.

Just as his arms were about to give out, Eric saw two bursts of white light hitting Varukan. One right in his chest, the other slicing through the tongue wrapped around him. Eric checked to see that it was indeed José. He had never been so happy to see his wide smile.

However, the face he saw was not the one he was familiar with. In fact, a lot of him was different. As José walked towards Eric, he began to see the various changes all over the bounty hunter's body. His face was obscured behind a silver mask with a bright yellow visor. His body was covered in navy blue skin adorned with golden stripes. On his chest was a massive golden star-shaped emblem.

He still wore gloves, boots, and holsters, each decorated with gold trimmings and a belt buckle. His hat had also changed to a shade of blue similar to his skin albeit with more gold stripes. Finally, his poncho had been replaced with a white cape, attached to his shoulders via a large golden band around his chest and back, held together with a single shoulder pad. The only thing that had not changed was the revolver. Eric recognized that this was no longer José. This was Star Slinger.

As he approached, Varukan got back up and lunged at Eric. With impressive speed, Star Slinger shot another blast at Varukan with incredible precision. As the menace agonized in pain, Star Slinger held out his hand to Eric. Understanding that the cowboy was once again concerned with his ally's well-being, Eric reached out. Grabbing his hand, Eric could feel his broken bones and bruises healing. But with so much focus on him, how much power did Star Slinger have to protect himself?

"Sorry I'm late, Eric. Took me a while to find you once I heard that blast. Kinda irresponsible for you to waste all your ammo on one shot."

Eric smiled, happy to hear his ally's patronizing, yet friendly tone. This was indeed still José.

"Sure, but it got your attention at least."

Varukan's pain-filled cries vanished from Eric's mind. The young man turned his attention back to the fallen foe and noticed a slow, grotesque change in the alien's physique. The invader growled viciously as his body swelled. First, the torso expanded to twice its previous size; then the arms elongated, followed by the legs. Its head grew in proportion to its newly expanded body. Then, cracks along its body began forming, like a dam ready to burst.

"You gotta get outta here!" shouted Star Slinger.

"Why, what's happening?"

"He's growing to full size. I'll be okay, but you'll be crushed."

Eric observed Varukan once more -- his body had expanded to three times its original size. The fractures now covered his entire body.

Suddenly, a welcome and familiar voice came through his DraCom. *"Hey, kid, I'm coming in for a landing. I have visuals of you and those two oddballs."*

Eric's eyes lit up with hope as the cavalry finally arrived. He could see Draco Azul flying in with incredible speed.

"Coach, am I glad to hear ya! The brown one's Varukan; the other's José's true form. Let loose Draco's scarf and don't land! Things are gonna get messy."

"One crimson scarf, coming right up!"

The metal goliath's lengthy cloth unwrapped around its neck as the mech flew parallel to the ground. As the scarf drifted over the streets of Guanajuato, Eric tossed Star Slinger's revolver back to its owner before he was scooped up by his mech.

With Eric wrapped in the safety of his mech's accessory, Star Slinger turned his attention back to Varukan. With a mighty outburst of power, the infamous slaughterer disposed of his diminutive layer of armor as it shattered into a million pieces. His new body elevated to unbelievable heights, rivaling that of Draco Azul. All the while, Star Slinger simply leered at his gigantic enemy, unfazed. The cowboy crossed his arms before thrusting them into the air. In that instance, his body encased itself in a ball of light and amplified its size before fading away, revealing a sixty-meter Star Slinger.

Both the bounty hunter and fugitive stared each other down, each preparing for the other to make his first move. Draco Azul, now controlled by Eric, landed behind Varukan, trapping him between his two enemies. Yet, judging by the wrongdoer's body language, he did not seem worried in the slightest. Rather, the monstrous alien seemed relaxed as he stood between the cowboy and the mech, even dispersing his signature laugh.

"The hell's with this guy?" a befuddled Ekchuah asked.

"You don't wanna know," Eric replied.

Varukan ceased his laughing before abruptly screaming in a high pitch that caused Star Slinger and Eric's minds to throb in pain once more. Eric fell to his hands and knees before noticing a familiar series of vines growing around him.

"Oh shoot!" was all he could shout before the Rozacdyl emerged from beneath the ground and enveloped Draco Azul in its thorny grip.

Distracted by his ally's situation, Star Slinger failed to notice Varukan striking the first blow. The two engaged in physical combat, exchanging kicks and punches at one another, all while the deadly outlaw gloated.

"You have to love this planet! For whatever reason, foreign beasts are attracted to this land. Finding one for myself was fairly easy with a little mind-bending."

Star Slinger found himself at a disadvantage. He was used to long-range combat, but he could not risk gaining space when there were so many fragile buildings around him. On top of that, transforming to giant size took a lot out of him, and any energy he would dispense from his guns would take an even greater toll on his body.

Varukan's incredible agility, while proportionally slower than his smaller form, still gave him the upper hand as he clamped onto Star Slinger's arms and threw him to the ground. The devilish fiend bashed Star Slinger's face repeatedly before checking back on his underling, watching it entrap the metal guardian's head within its jaws.

The Rozacdyl and I have a connection. Like me, it's a survivor. A creature that does what is necessary to carry out its ultimate goal: dominance and satisfaction. Together, nothing can stand in our way!

All of a sudden, the Rozacdyl screeched in pain. Its head caught on fire as it was consumed by lightning. The beast loosened its grip as it tried to escape, but Eric would not allow it. He had dealt with this thing once and was determined to end its existence, this time for good. He grappled the monstrosity and lifted its entire body over Draco Azul's head. The Rozacdyl thrashed its body and lashed out at the mech, again and again, clawing and slashing its armor.

Eric's body felt every instance of damage the Diablo inflicted, but tried to endure until his final resort was ready.

No! Varukan shouted.

With his panicked opponent's grip loosening, Star Slinger slipped his arm out and grabbed one of his revolvers, aiming it at the criminal's gut. Several fires were all it took to turn the tables.

Star Slinger grabbed ahold of his weakened enemy and forced him to watch his pet's annihilation. "This time, *you'll* feel the very pain you have wreaked across the entire galaxy!"

Within the cockpit of the Primal Warrior, Eric was reaching his limits as his body was struggling to maintain its strength against the Diablo's pummeling.

"You're at max power, Eric -- Go for it!" Ekchuah shouted as he gave the signal.

"Draco Strikeeeeer!"

Lightning burst from Draco Azul's horn, five times stronger than his previous attempt. The Rozacdyl's body was consumed by the thunderous display, and so too was any hope of its longevity. Its entire being crumbled away like dust in the wind.

Nearby, a compromised Varukan fell terribly silent. Star Slinger believed that his will to fight had vanished.

"Now, you know what it's like to lose something precious to you."

Oh, do I now?

Surprised by his enemy's words, he quickly noticed his two tongues speeding towards him from behind. It was apparent he had regrown his amputated organs during his transformation. Star Slinger jumped and dodged the attack, but not before the deadly mouthpieces destroyed both revolvers within their holsters.

You arrogant fool. As if I could ever consider another being with compassion. That creature was nothing more than a tool. The only one worthy of my affection is myself!

Varukan lashed out with his spearing tongues, each one landing a critical hit on Star Slinger's body. Quickly, one tongue pierced through his shoulder. Gushes of silver blood oozed from his wounds. Eric, still exhausted from his last attack, marched forward to aid his friend. Varukan witnessed the robot heading his way and threw his second appendage right through Draco Azul's abdomen.

"Gah!" Eric uttered in pain.

"Kid!"

Varukan laughed as he mocked his adversaries.

Emotions like love and compassion are for the weak. You two fight for each other and look where that's gotten you. It's simply idiotic!

"Don't be so sure!" Star Slinger rebutted.

Varukan heard a metal clamp and noticed Draco Azul grasping onto his tongue with both hands. Slowly he pulled the menace towards him.

What could you possibly be doing? Varukan scoffed as he struggled to maintain his distance. *You don't have the strength to challenge me.*

"For someone who looks down on others, you have a bad habit of repeating your mistakes," Eric said. "Guess some people never learn."

What are you blabbering on about!

"He's talking about this!" the bounty hunter exclaimed.

Varukan turned his attention on Star Slinger, now pulling a secret weapon from behind his belt. It was the small leather-clad rod from before. From the shaft, a soft blue light emerged before solidifying into a wide outlandish blade matching his gold and navy-blue colors.

"I got this as a reward from my last bounty. Normally I prefer my firearms, but I guess I can make an exception for you."

He sliced Varukan's tongue in half and ran towards the nefarious foe. The alien monstrosity tried to escape, but his remaining appendage was caught in the hands of the azure robot who was now running towards him with the last of his strength.

With a single thrust, Draco Azul's arm blade wedged into Varukan's back armor plates, keeping him in place as Star Slinger lifted his sword in the air. With a single swing, the desperado cleaved his enemy in half, right down the middle.

For a brief second, Eric could hear the most agonized and terrified scream he had ever heard before it was abruptly silenced. A cathartic part of him felt glad to have heard such a despicable creature's dying thoughts.

As the two halves of the former wanted criminal collapsed, his tongues fell limp to the ground before his entire being exploded like a set of fireworks.

"Um, what was that?" Eric asked as he attempted to speak with his bruised and battered chest.

"His species is known," Star Slinger responded with heavy breathing, "for their explosive blood upon expiration."

Eric stood there dumbfounded at the revelation. Though eventually, he decided it was best to surrender to the absurdity of his situation.

"Oh… okay."

***

The sun rose to a city scarred by last night's war. Its citizens swarmed the areas where giants once battled. First responders provided emergency medical care for the victims who lost their homes, businesses, and loved ones. Meanwhile, policemen did their best to hold back the various journalists scrambling to get the big scoop, social influencers recording their experiences for maximum views, and curious passersby who simply wanted to know what had transpired.

Meanwhile, far from the city within the hot arid valley laid the Primal Warrior, recovering from yesterday's battle. As its self-repair systems mended its mechanical scars, a bandaged Eric stepped out of his mech to bid farewell to José, who had reverted back to his human form to heal from his own wounds. Once more, Ekchuah refused to allow him inside the mech as Eric rested. Despite their bodies being weathered, worn, and beaten, both fighters smiled at one another.

"I'm glad to see you're alright, Eric," José spoke. "I wanted to check up on you once more before I head off."

The smile on Eric faded. While he was initially put off by the overly optimistic foreigner, he had grown to like his new ally. Perhaps even consider him a friend.

"Wait, what do you mean?"

"I have to report Varukan's demise to the authorities. Then I'll be off on another bounty. There are far more heinous beings in the galaxy, and I swear I will exterminate as many as possible so long as I live!" It was apparent that José's strength and enthusiasm had already returned in full force since their fight.

"B-but, what about these alien monsters invading Earth? Surely, something's gotta be done about it."

"Of course, there's clearly some mysterious force at play here on this planet, and that's where *you* come in," the cowboy said, harkening back to his initial conversation with Eric the previous day.

"Hey, listen! I can't do this on my own. I'm not a hero. I-I'm just a guy with a robot."

José placed a firm hand on Eric's shoulder. The young man stood quiet.

"That's exactly *why* you're a hero, Eric. Your humility and selflessness are what make you a prime guardian in my book!" José said as he flashed a grin and a thumbs up at him.

"While you certainly have a lot of learning to do," the bounty hunter continued, "I'm confident the Earth is already in good hands. Meanwhile, there are plenty of other planets out there in need of my help. And that's the responsibility I've chosen to partake, as you have with your mech."

Eric could not think of anything to say. His mind was always plagued with self-doubt, unsure if he could ever keep his planet safe from whatever was sending out Diablos. However, to hear such words of encouragement from someone he learned to deeply respect, this was something he truly needed to hear, even if he himself was not consciously aware of it yet.

"I guess… if you ever need any help, you know where to find me."

"I most certainly will, my friend. Take care, and let justice prevail!"

The cowboy then crossed his arms and began to illuminate his signature white aura. It was so bright Eric had trouble keeping his eyes open. Through his hand, he could witness the aura that was José lift off into the sky. Higher and higher he ascended until he was presumably soaring across the stars.

"See ya, space cowboy," whispered Eric as he waved his injured hand at the sky.

Only, his arm was not in pain. In fact, he barely felt any pain at all throughout his body. Did José heal him one last time? Despite their short time together, Eric was going to miss the odd fellow. If anything, it was good to know he was not the only one out there fighting the good fight. Still, with his new friend off in the depths of space, Eric found himself becoming Earth's last hope once more, a burden he wished he did not have to carry alone.

END

DRACO AZUL: REMINISCENCE

A storm raged late at night in the jungles of the Yukatan Peninsula. Normally a massive tourist attraction, the Maya site Calakmul was populated by the local wildlife, as well as a massive guest that once roamed this land long ago. Thunderous clouds and heavy winds deafened the rainfall as bolts of lightning streaked across the sky.

One particular bolt of nature's electrical vipers flashed toward one of the many towering archeological marvels in the area. Rather than striking the massive pyramid, it instead attacked the structure right next to it. Unlike the temple, it was metal in nature. The lightning was absorbed into the gigantic complex.

The structure attracted more bolts as it became electrostatic. Several strikes aimed at the long, thin portion that claimed the top of the structure, like that of a lightning rod on a man-made building. If any man, woman, or child were to witness this flurry of discharges from the heavens and were privy to the recent ongoings in Mexico, they could tell you without a doubt that the colossal object that stood next to the pyramid was none other than the heroic robot, Draco Azul.

For the first few months of Eric Martinez's crusade against the Diablos, he and his artificial intelligent mentor, Ekchuah, would hide their blue mech within the mountains of Sierra Madre del Sur, and wait until the next assault. However, since witnessing an attack firsthand in Ensenada, Eric decided to no longer remain in one single location. Instead, he believed it was best to move from place to place, hunting down any monsters that may already be in hiding, such as the plant-like creature in Durango City. For Eric, this was far more preferable than waiting for destruction to unfold at a potentially far off location.

In the meantime, he would continue training, refining his skills until he had mastered the fantastic power of his ancient extraterrestrial machine. Recently, his digital teacher advised him to find shelter in a spot where they would be able to replenish Draco Azul's strength. As great as the machine was, it was not a self-sustaining invention. Under the direction of Ekchuah, the pilot had relocated his mammoth instrument of justice within the northern Petén Basin region, an area Ekchuah became very familiar with during Draco Azul's heyday as a symbol of the Maya people. Here, the bladed titan would absorb the storm's lightning, thereby refueling its energy reserves and kick its nanotech repair systems into high gear.

During this time, Eric had engaged Ekchuah in yet another sparring session. Despite being nothing more than a computer-generated hologram, Ekchuah was able to simulate the feeling of touch through Eric's skin-tight pilot suit that covered his entire body. Ekchuah let loose strike after strike, keeping Eric on his toes.

"Keep your mind sharp, kid!" Ekchuah instructed. "Look for any possible openings."

It was difficult for Eric to constantly avoid his instructor's punches, let alone concentrate enough on any weak spots.

Then, he realized it. All this time Ekchuah was putting his focus into his arms and not his legs. The young man attempted to sweep his trainer's limbs, but before his attack could land, Ekchuah leaped off the ground. By the time Eric regained his footing, it was already too late. The AI figure came down hard with a swift chop to Eric's neck, knocking him out.

As soon as Eric regained consciousness, he was greeted by the voice of his tutor.

"Sharp eye you got there, kid, but we gotta work on that timing of yours."

"As if I'm ever gonna fight someone as good as you," joked Eric as he got back up.

"Oh, you'd be surprised. It's a big world out there and an even bigger universe."

"Let me guess, your past students ended up fighting some pretty nasty foes?" Eric said half-heartedly.

"What, you don't believe me?" the holographic coach asked as he raised an eyebrow.

"No, not at all! It's just that… well… given all the craziness we've been through, it's just… I don't know, kinda hard to imagine it myself."

Eric could see Ekchuah's face grow even more upset. This look always gave Eric the heebie-jeebies. The last thing he wanted to do was piss Ekchuah off.

"L-look, don't get me wrong! I'm sure you and Draco have seen some stuff in the past. I just don't know how to prepare myself for that."

Ekchuah listened to his pupil's words and thought about them. The AI muttered to himself as would a real person in a state of conflict.

"Hard to imagine huh? Don't know how to prepare…" The hologram then snapped his fingers, only they failed to make any sort of sound due to their intangible nature.

"Tell ya what, kid, you wanna see what we've been through? I'll just show ya myself!"

"W-what?" Eric was bewildered. Just what on Earth was his coach thinking?

Ekchuah activated the mechanical arms that sprung forth from the walls and ceiling, each appendage holding a piece of Eric's suit for controlling Draco Azul.

"What's gonna happen? Are we gonna time travel to the past or something?"

"Hah, now that's funny, kid! What do you think this is, science-fiction? Nah, it's what you humans call these days 'Virtual Reality.' I wasn't sure if you'd be ready for this, but I think you can handle it."

Virtual reality? Is he serious? thought Eric. While the technology within his giant robot had surpassed his wildest dreams, he always saw virtual reality as an impossible dream that had since been relegated to a novelty for video games. Then again, he was currently talking to a computer system as if it were a living breathing person within a gigantic robot.

"Alright, coach. Hook me up, or whatever it is you need to do."

"That's the spirit!"

Ekchuah then had the arm and leg gauntlets attach to Eric's limbs, followed by the chest and backplates. Finally, came the helmet which obscured his sense of sight within the cockpit. The pilot was accustomed to wearing these accessories whenever it was time to get behind the wheel of the Primal Warrior. Each time he did so, Draco Azul's body became his -- every sensation, be it sight, touch, or even pain, Eric would feel the appropriate equivalent. *Was all of this really going to work in a VR environment?*

"Get ready, kid. Activating mission one!"

The dark visor within Eric's helmet was instantly brightened with a shiny blue aura. Suddenly, Eric was surrounded by what could only be described as an aqua blue void that expanded endlessly all around him. He looked down at his hands and saw that he was once again possessed the body of Draco Azul. Only this time it felt different. He felt a lot lighter. The few steps he took did not cause any vibrations around him.

"Is Draco moving outside?" Eric asked.

"Nope, it's just you this time," Ekchuah's voice echoed within the void. "Don't worry, I'm currently calibrating your body's movements within the system, so it'll feel as real as possible. Once that's done the environment will load from Draco's memory banks."

After a few more seconds, the environment around Eric morphed into a land filled with trees, bushes, grass, and a wide-open field. On one side of the field was a beautiful beach with sand as white as snow, and a translucent blue ocean you could practically see through. On the other side, was a luscious green forest that seemed to stretch on forever.

The next element to load were people, mostly men, working together to build some sort of establishment within their sixteen-acre land. However, there was something significantly different about these people. They did not appear to be modern Mexicans. Their skin looked bronze, almost copper in color, and their hair was as black as the night sky. The men wore little more than loincloths and hip-cloths. Some with simple color palettes and patterns, while others were plain white.

The women, on the other hand, wore dresses and skirts with similarly varying degrees of colors and designs. They were in charge of cultivating the land for future harvest seasons. It became apparent to Eric that what he was looking at was a recreation of a small portion of the Maya civilization.

"Woah," was all Eric could say upon the realization that he was witnessing a lost culture that many generations had studied but could never fully grasp.

He himself was always fascinated with the native roots of his own ancestry as far back as the fourth grade when he studied Mesoamerican culture. It was this interest that led him to pursue Anthropology through a Social Studies major and eventually become a high school teacher. He never thought in a million years that he would be able to see the Maya people firsthand.

"What are they doing?" he asked and began to hear Ekchuah's voice reverberate all around him.

"They're currently building what would become one of the most ambitious cities in the Yukatan Peninsula, Tulum -- a coastal town that was protected by twelve-meter tall seaside cliffs on one side, and a wall over seven hundred meters in length covering every other side!" the AI proudly boasted.

"Tulum, huh?" the pilot said as he began to rub his chin, before realizing he was making his simulated version of Draco Azul perform the same action.

At that moment, it dawned on him. He was out in the open.

"Wait a minute!" he exclaimed. "What's Draco doing out here? Shouldn't we be hiding?"

"Don't worry kid," Ekchuah calmly answered, "At this point in time, the locals have gotten used to Draco's existence. Sure, we still kept the pilots' identities a secret for the safety of them and their families, but everyone here knows we're not a threat. In fact, they requested our assistance."

"Assistance? Like, to build the city?"

"Nah, they're more than capable of doing that on their own. It's what you're about to go up against that's the problem."

Eric grew a look of concern on his face.

"You see, a while after this colony began construction, their people mysteriously disappeared on two occasions. Once they started believing this land was cursed, they reached out to us over in Chichen Itza. For your first mission, you're playing bodyguard for these nice folks."

"So… when's the threat gonna show up?"

As if in reply, a massive splash of water viciously struck the cliffs.

"Does that answer your question?" replied the sarcastic mentor.

Creeping from behind the largest cliff were several red tentacles. Each appendage was covered in a rough and slimy texture. More tentacles surfaced as they squirmed their way throughout the city. Each arm swayed left and right as if they were feeling out for something in particular. Several of the men and women were trapped in the limbs of the mysterious invader while others attempted to flee.

"That's your cue, kid!" advised Ekchuah.

Eric shook his head and sprung into action. He made his robotic avatar jump over the entire city and landed on the shores behind the cliffs. There he witnessed the perpetrator of the attack, a gigantic octopus. Like something out of the legends of sea-faring travelers, the animal was larger than any cephalopod known to man and was most certainly hungry for human flesh.

"Is this thing native to Earth?" asked a perplexed Eric.

"Yup. Like I said, there's much to this world you humans still aren't aware of. This creature, or the 'Devilfish' as the locals called it, normally laid at the bottom of the sea, but every once in a while, one would come up to the surface in search of new prey. That is, of course, until *we* took care of it." Eric could sense the cockiness coming out of the prideful voice of his mentor.

He then focused his attention back on the Devilfish and went in for the kill. But before Eric could strike the beast's head with a single punch, several tentacles lashed out and wrapped themselves around Draco Azul's arm. Normally, the mech's blades would cut into the flesh of any living being it made contact with. However, in the case of the Devilfish's limbs, the razor-weapons barely left a mark on their thick and rubbery skin as they squeezed around his arm.

In Eric's confusion, two more arms grappled the Primal Warrior's legs with enough force to pull the giant robot off its feet. Eric fell on his backside, with now three of his limbs ensnared by the octopus. The aquatic monstrosity held its prey over its head with its remaining three tentacles. The pilot struggled to pull his arm and legs free to no avail. He even sent out his crimson scarf to wrestle with the monster's limbs, only for it to become ensnared in the behemoth's grasp.

What was he to do? Should he unleash a lightning strike? No, that would harm the natives. Should he strike the Devilfish with his remaining arm? No can do, the animal could easily use its remaining limbs to stop him and further harm its hostages.

Suddenly the entire simulation froze. The Devilfish and innocent bystanders were all trapped in a state of limbo. Once more, Eric heard the voice of his teacher.

"Here's a perfect opportunity to try out a new technique."

A three-dimensional display of Draco Azul's entire body showed up on Eric's display. He noticed that the model of his machine was raising its fists. The blades removed themselves from its forearms. There he noticed a handle on each blade, to which the model grabbed onto and formed a fighting position with each blade in hand.

"A-are those--?"

"Yes, indeed! You're looking at a means of increasing your attack range at the cost of hand-to-hand combat. Introducing the *Draco Fangs!* Just shout out the phrase and the systems will recognize your vocal input."

The 3-D model disappeared, and the simulation resumed before Eric even had a chance to comprehend his new ability. The closest thing to a weapon he ever held was a kitchen knife, a dubious claim at best. He could not see himself doing well holding a massive blade, let alone two of them. Still, what other choice did he have? He took a deep breath as he always did and hoped for the best.

"Draco Fangs!" he shouted. The blade on his right arm stayed attached due to its compromised position while the other blade shot up into the air. Eric's hesitation caused him to miss the blade as it came down, stabbing into the sandy shore.

"Damn it!" cursed Eric.

"Don't worry, you'll get the hang of it. That's why we're here. Now grab your blade and kick its ass!"

Ekchuah's pupil did just as he was told. With Draco Azul's hand, he grabbed onto the razor-sharp weapon and pulled it out of the ground like he was King Arthur heaving the legendary Excalibur from its pedestal. He lifted the weapon over his head and threw it down at the three tentacles that were latched onto his right arm. The force of the razor-sharp sword was enough to slice through the Devilfish's appendages, leaving them to hang off the mech's arm.

Eric looked up to realize that it was now waving its victims back and forth as its remaining arms flailed around wildly in pain. Eric reached out to the tentacles in the hopes of saving the people but was blinded by a spray of ink launched by the invertebrate.

Though caught off guard, Eric could feel the octopus letting go of its grip on his mech's legs. It was then that he realized that it must be trying to escape with its meal in tow. Eric tried to listen for where the creature was moving as he rubbed ink from his machine's optical sensors.

Through a blurry vision and the sound of suckers squirming across the sand, he could tell the Devilfish was just about to enter the water. Draco Azul grabbed onto its scarf, twirled it like a lasso, and launched it at the overgrown mollusk. Though tied by the cloth, its slimy skin allowed the Devilfish to slowly escape its grip. However, it was not quick enough as the scarf bought Eric barely enough time for him to lunge at the monster and stab it directly between the eyes.

With one swipe, Eric grabbed onto all three limbs with his newly freed arm. He pulled his weapon out of the dying animal and cut the people free. With the Maya villagers in his hand, he walked back towards Tulum to set them down. There, the remaining people who managed to escape the Devilfish's wrath cheered at the victorious metal titan.

Eric turned to see his foe one last time to confirm its demise.

"Looks like they're having sushi tonight," Eric said as he smiled.

"Nice goin', champ. Not bad for a first-timer."

Eric drew his attention back onto Tulum one last time before the simulation ended. He could see the city and its people fade back into the memory banks of Draco Azul.

"Do you and Draco have any memories of Tulum after its completion?" asked Eric.

"Sorry, kid. Me and Draco went into retirement just before it was finished. We... never got to see the whole thing come together. And... given what happened to the Maya, we never will." Eric could detect a solemn tone in Ekchuah's voice as he reflected on the lost city.

He remembered a similar situation soon after he first met Ekchuah. It was during his first training sessions that he noticed his instructor exploring the Internet so as to update himself on the 800 years that had transpired since Draco Azul went into hibernation. It was there that he discovered the ultimate fate of the Maya along with the other Mesoamerican civilizations.

At the time he shrugged it off, believing it was no use worrying over the past when Mexico was currently in trouble. Yet, given the AI's ties to the Maya, right down to his hologram's appearance, Eric always felt that Ekchuah was hiding more than he was letting on. It was at this moment that his suspicions were confirmed.

"Hey, coach... Ekchuah. Do you ever... miss them?"

"Yeah, guess you can say that. Met plenty of amazing people back then. But that's the thing about life, kid. Things change. Nothing ever stays the same, ya know? Plus, nothing can be done about the past. It's the future we should always focus on." Ekchuah's voice regained his confidence upon reciting those last words.

"Now that the practice round is done, let's get started on your *real* challenge!"

Eric could imagine the grin on Ekchuah's face as he foreshadowed his next VR mission. He was not sure whether to smile as well or grimace.

A few seconds later and the blue techno void was replaced by a large forest, this time surrounding Eric on all sides. He looked all around confusingly at what he needed to focus on, until he saw a large caravan walking by his feet. Through his telescopic vision, he noticed they were carrying handwoven backpacks that held various items. The most peculiar feature was the black paint these travelers wore all over their bodies.

"Who are these people?" the pilot asked.

"They're merchants from Tikal, Calakmul, and a few other places, all on their way towards the great city of Teotihuacan. They were vital in the structure of Maya society. Through the trading and selling of cacao, art, jewelry, clothing, food, and especially obsidian, they maintained a healthy relationship between their numerous cities. These guys here are in it for the long haul. Merchants like these were considered the elite, the best of the best!"

Once more, Eric was mesmerized by the site of the Mesoamerican entrepreneurs. Though he studied Maya culture at multiple points in his education, he was not familiar with their body paint.

"What's with the full-body makeup?"

"Long-distance routes are always the most dangerous. They believed travels like these are like a walk through the underworld, a land of the dead. And during this period, it got really bad."

"So, lemme guess, we're here to investigate?"

"Now you're getting it!" Ekchuah cheerfully stated.

Eric slowly trailed behind the twenty-member band of merchants for the next thirty minutes, occasionally stepping ahead to look out for any potential threats only to see nothing but more forest and wildlife. He was becoming impatient as time passed. He initially expected to be thrown into the heat of battle just as before. Was this the test Ekchuah planned? His teacher would not say; he kept silent throughout the journey, possibly observing Eric's skills as a protector.

During this trek, he thought about Draco Azul's role in this society. Was this really what it was like for past pilots to come to people's aid back then? How many unfortunate souls had to die before a messenger could finally travel to wherever the mech was stationed in order to request its help? Eric realized how fortunate he was that his constant access to the Internet was what allowed him to detect any major trouble the moment it began. *And the old geezers thought technology would destroy society*, he amusingly thought.

As he walked, he began to notice a thick blanket of fog obscuring his vision. It was bizarre to witness such a drastic shift from the clear sunny weather. In fact, he could not see the merchants below him. *Was this what was killing travelers?*

"Everyone stay put!" he ordered. He was thankful Ekchuah set the language of this simulation to English, the only thing he explained during the long walk here.

His sensors picked up the sounds of the merchants ceasing their march. He activated his infrared vision, another one of the numerous options that enhanced Eric's sight. With it, he could detect twenty human outlines. As he lowered down to pick them up, he caught sight of a cold entity through his robot's thermal imaging cameras. It was massive and drifted right above the trees before whizzing around the Primal Warrior. Eric tried to keep track of it, but it was moving too fast. He was spinning in circles at that point.

He stopped himself before he lost his balance. Still reeling from slight nausea, he heard the sound of something running. Something big. Before he could react, he was attacked by a blast of fire. Eric turned in the direction of his mysterious attacker, only to see nothing but the chilling fog. He quickly remembered the merchants. It was too dangerous for them to be near here.

"Scatter! Run as far away from here. I'll take care of this!"

The men did as they were told and separated into several groups, running in all directions. Immediately several of them were snatched off the ground by the icy entity.

"No!" was all Eric could shout before being attacked by another fireball.

The attacker came at him with several strikes and kicks. Whatever this was, it was humanoid in shape. It was like sparring with Ekchuah.

"Die, False Idol!" shouted the attacker before sending two more fireballs at Draco Azul.

It can talk? Just what exactly was he up against? Whatever it was, it was sentient and intelligent.

"You're strong, False Idol. But your power is nothing compared to a god!" The figure hiding in the fog let out a loud eerie cackle, high and thin in tone.

"A *what*?" Eric responded in disbelief.

"Ah! So, you're not only a False Idol but a non-believer as well? How ironic!"

The sneering figure then summoned bright flames, though not for attacking. This fire was to dispel the fog surrounding him to reveal his true form.

"Seeing as how you managed to survive so far, I shall reward you with my presence."

Eric turned off his thermal vision to get a better view of what he was looking at. To his disbelief, it was a walking, talking skeleton, surrounded by green flames. The skeletal being dressed like a royal Maya priest, with a headdress made of black wilted feathers, a dull golden pectoral collar, equally dulled wrist & leg bands, and an old, tattered skirt.

Its empty eye sockets glowed intensely with the same green light that emanated from his aura.

"Allow me to introduce myself. I am known by many names, but you shall call me Hunhau: Lord of the Valley of Death, Master of the Dark Flames, and Devourer of Souls!"

"Alright, time out. Ekchuah!" Eric shouted into the sky before the simulation halted once more.

"What do you need?" Ekchuah nonchalantly responded.

"What do I need? How about an explanation as to what this 'god' is or where it even came from?" Just then, Eric's eyes widened.

"Hold on, is the entire Maya pantheon real? Are any of the other culture's gods real?"

"Woah, woah, woah, slow down kid!" the AI said as he tried to calm down his exasperated student. "Geez, you sleep for a few centuries and already everyone forgets about the gods. I honestly didn't think you'd react this way given how many gods you humans still worship these days.

"And to answer your next question: no, I don't know whether or not your modern gods exist. I did my research and if they're real they seem to operate much differently than the guys we dealt with. As far as I know, they're a mystery. Now, as for these past gods, yes. They all existed in one form or another. However, Draco and I mainly had beef with what you humans would call the 'Mesoamerican Gods.'"

"A-are they, like... *actual* gods?" Eric said under his trembling breath.

"If you're asking if they're the creators of the whole goddamn universe like they claim to be, no. What they actually are is a hyper-evolved species of aliens. From the data I've gathered over the centuries, their birth rate is exceedingly low as their long lifespans and ever-increasing power made reproduction obsolete. Over the course of a god's lifespan, they find the one natural force that suits them and base their whole identity around it. They can also adopt any form they so choose over time. Sometimes they're humanoid, other times not.

"Their main form of consumption is by absorbing the life force given off by their worshipers. The tighter the bonds are between them and their followers, the stronger they got."

Eric stood there in shock and awe as he took all this world-shattering information in.

"In the case of our undead buddy, he specialized in forcefully draining energy from organisms, like a vampire. Long ago he invented a technique that allowed him to rob victims until they were nothing but dry husks. This allowed him to weaponize their life force into what he calls his 'Dark Flames.' That's how he ended up with the title of God of Death.

"He and his brother tried to become the head honchos among the other gods but ended up getting their butts kicked and were forced to live down on Earth. That's where the whole 'Underworld' myth came from. It wasn't underneath the Earth that was his domain; it was beneath the heavens, or at least beneath the portal that led to the gods' domain. A pocket dimension of sorts. Ya got all that, kid?"

Eric slowly nodded, still trying to reel in the fact that not only did his universe contain horrific monsters both native and foreign to his planet, but also godly beings that at one point had been worshipped by man. And here he thought it could not get any stranger than the Diablos.

"Y-yeah. So, what happened to them? I mean, *all* of them?"

"Well, me, Draco, and my former pilots did our best to keep the Mesoamerican gods at bay. Once we retired, though, we left it up to the locals to take over from there. As for the gods in other parts of the world, we figured the humans had a handle on things, hence why Draco and I stayed here. After all, our creators must've left us here for a reason. Once Draco and I woke up in the modern age, we found no record of them for the last millennia. I assumed they must've left Earth once humans no longer worshipped them. Now, is *that* it?"

"I think so. Wait, did you say this guy had a brother?"

"Whoops! Uh, spoilers?" Ekchuah cheekily replied before quickly starting the simulation back up.

Eric had no time to ponder about this revelation as he now had to face this blast from the past. The God of Death immediately resumed his pompous speech.

"From the moment those mysterious fools bestowed upon you humans that ridiculous suit of armor, you have disturbed the natural order and earned our ire in the process."

"Mysterious fools?" He must be talking about Draco's creators. Were those aliens "gods" as well, or something else entirely?

"I knew my actions would lure you to my domain sooner or later, and once I eliminate you, my rivals will have no choice but to crown me their ruler!"

While he had no facial muscles, Eric could detect sadistic giddiness in the deity's voice. This god was anxious to fight him.

"Now, will you accept your fate and fall by my hand? Or, will you die a warrior's death? Regardless, I shall be victorious, for a god can never be bested by a mortal, regardless of their weapon!"

Eric had heard enough of his incessant pontifications.

"Alright, Billy Bones. You're asking for it now!"

"Insolent cretin! You shall refer to me as--"

"I don't care!" As Eric shouted, he raised his arms and uttered his new voice command.

"Draco Fangs!"

The blades jumped out of their slots within the mech's forearms, taking the god by surprise.

"Oh no, you don't!"

Hunhau swiped his arm in front of him, discharging five smaller Dark Flame projectiles at the giant robot. Eric was too focused on grabbing his blades out of the air for him to notice the Dark Flames. Once he seized his weapons his eyes caught glimpse of the fire coming right at him. His mind reacted quicker than his body, allowing his subconscious thoughts to manipulate Draco Azul's scarf into defending the metal titan. To his amazement, the scarf took no damage.

Woah, how strong is this thing? Eric wondered to himself.

"Impossible! Nothing can stop my Dark Flames," the bewildered god shouted.

"Yeah? Well, sorry to disappoint you," replied Eric as he raised his sabers in a new makeshift battle stance. "You're going down!"

The death god's forearms were now encased in his emerald fire. "We shall see about that, False Idol."

Hunhau released a bombardment of jade-colored comets at the azure robot. Too many for one single scarf to block. Eric jumped out of the way and kept moving as the barrage continued. Eric reactivated his thermal vision to keep track of the skeleton's scorching body within the thick fog.

The Devourer of Souls leaped into the air to increase his range, raining hell to the jungles around Draco Azul. Eric thought of the merchants still in hiding. With the god falling back down to the ground, Eric began charging electrostatic energy and aimed it at where he was going to land.

Before he could begin to recite his attack's vocal command, he was struck from behind. The pilot screamed as he felt claws digging into his back and forcing him to the ground.

What was that just now? It could not have been the god since Eric was keeping track of it the whole time. It had to be a second enemy.

As he got back up, he felt a strange numbness in his back. It was a cold sensation. Also, moments before the impact he could have sworn he heard a screeching sound. That was when Eric remembered the sub-zero specter that was darting around the fog.

"It wasn't the skeleton," Eric said under his breath, "it was his brother!"

"See if you can avoid this, foolish mortal!" Hunhau shouted as he shot larger blasts of his Dark Flames.

Eric could not afford to move around in the event that the brother would attack him at the worst possible moment. He crossed his blades to form a makeshift shield. The bombs landed and Draco Azul was still in one piece, though his blades were heavily scathed. The deity continued to throw projectiles, seeing the robot struggling to keep standing.

With Eric's arms and legs on the verge of giving out, he heard that same screech, like that of a demonic bird of prey. Quick to respond this time, Draco Azul's scarf looped in front of the mech and grabbed one of Hunhau's bombs. Miraculously, it remained burning in the folds of the powerful cloth.

Eric instructed his scarf to launch it in the direction of the second attacker's cries. He heard an explosion, followed by a higher pitch screech and a massive thud.

"Brother!" cried the death god.

The pilot took this opportunity to rush forward and stabbed at the skeletal menace with both blades. Draco Azul's mighty arms raised its twin sabers and lifted the dark lord over its head and threw him at his ally.

All around Eric the thick fog was disappearing, and the sun was shining once again on the jungle. The young man quickly scanned the whole area with his normal telescopic vision, only to find half of the merchants dead. The rest remained in hiding, now in smaller groups.

Was it the other god that did this? His frustration at his failure to protect them grew into rage. Rage aimed squarely at the demonic pair.

"Who the hell is that?" demanded Eric, raising a sword at them both. The skeletal god got back up on his feet, his shattered ribs slowly reforming. *Must be one of the perks of being a god*, thought Eric.

"He is none other than my brother, my sole ally in my quest to become a god amongst gods: *Uacmitun Ahau!*"

The mass beside him looked like a mound of black feathers that gave off a dark, smokey aura. The mass twisted and shifted before it too began to rise. The feathers were not his body per se, but a massive cloak that completely shrouded the god's body save for his grey scaley hands, each adorned with razor talons. His face, hiding underneath a hood, was skeletal just like his brother. However, it was not a humanoid skull; rather, it was birdlike instead. No light shined from these eye sockets. Peering into his nonexistent eyes, Eric could only find a pure void of shadow.

Uacmitun Ahau opened his beak, but rather than speaking, the death god let out the same animalistic battle cry Eric heard when it attacked him.

"So, I take it you're the brains between the two of you?"

"Do not insult Uacmitun Ahau!" Hunhau objected. "He has no need for words and is as equally powerful and intelligent as I! His methods merely differ from my own. It was his shroud of darkness that allowed us to trap you and your followers. And he would have decided your fate had it not been for your confounded scheme."

Both Hunhau and his brother prepared to continue their fight. The skeleton's Dark Flames returned, and the bird's black smoke intensified.

"Together, our abilities make us the perfect team to destroy you and become--"

"Yeah, yeah. The king of gods," Eric interrupted, having heard this spiel before.

"God of gods, you impudent mortal!" The light in Hunhau's eyes fiercely sparked.

"I swear, if it were not for your puzzling gift from beyond, you wouldn't be so confident. It is a power far too great for such an unworthy species! We will be sure to remove you from your armor, expose you for the fraudulent human that you are, and give you a death most slow and torturous!"

The deathly brothers leapt at Draco Azul. Eric, ready to retaliate, did his best to dodge his opponent's attacks while studying their movements. Uacmitun Ahau resorted to using his claws, while Hunhau switched to using his Dark Flame-enchanted fists. Each brother threw a ravenous cavalcade of swipes and strikes at the Primal Warrior. That was when Eric was ready to strike back.

"Draco Wings!"

With his wings fully activated, Draco Azul took off into the sky. Taking a page from a previous battle in Mexico City, Eric had the metal giant's scarf wrap around Hunhau's waist. Before the talkative deity could utter a single word, his body was forcefully whisked away with the mech.

Higher and higher the robot flew, all while the god struggled to free himself from the cloth's grip. Trailing behind the pair was the vulture of death coming to his brother's rescue. Draco Azul lowered its head to inspect the situation. Eric was now ready to spring his plan into action.

Draco Azul placed each blade back into their respective slots and stopped in place. It grabbed onto the scarf that held its foe prisoner and tilted its wings at an angle that allowed it to quickly revolve like a spinning top. The circular motion left Hunhau helpless and screaming for his sibling as he was swung around like an astronaut in a G-force machine. Uacmitun Ahau screeched in rage as he readied his talons and closed the distance between him and his enemy.

At that moment, Draco Azul aimed his divine adversary at just the right angle and let go of Hunhau. The speed at which he was flung caused him to slam down into the avian creature, resulting in the brothers tumbling back down to Earth. At that moment, Draco Azul gathered energy into its central horn once more.

"Let's speed up that landing a bit. Draco Striker!"

A beam of lightning exploded from the Primal Warrior's horn at a velocity far greater than the falling gods. The beam reached the gods and not only accelerated their descent, but also inflicted great pain. The moment of impact and the resulting eruption of the attack's energy created a massive crater that wiped out all living things nearby. The jungle caught on fire in the aftermath of the lightning-filled explosion. As Draco Azul descended down to inspect its nemesis, Eric heard his mentor's voice for the first time since his lowdown on the gods.

"Eric, look at what you did! You gotta pay attention to your surroundings."

"What do you mean? We're in the middle of a jungle?" The pupil angrily protested.

"Exactly! Not only are you destroying the very routes the Maya use to travel, but you're also killing off the vegetation and wildlife. Not to mention the poor merchants."

Upon realizing what he might have done, the student cursed under his breath. Had he really been that nearsighted? Once he landed his mech he checked for the survivors of the caravan; he searched all around the area, but they were nowhere to be found. He called out to the group but picked up no responses. It was getting harder to see as the flames grew. His thermal vision was useless in this situation.

"Impressive. Most impressive," a familiar voice teased.

Eric turned to find Hunhau, beaten and battered, escaping what should have been his tomb. The skeletal giant observed the destruction his foe inadvertently caused, then faced the mech itself.

"Despite proclaiming to be a defender, you're equally as adept to be a destroyer. Perhaps... even better."

"S-shut up! You don't know anything about me!" Eric shouted, allowing his emotions to fall victim to his challenger's mocking.

"Oh, I can tell what sort of person you are, False Idol. You are like us, beings filled with hatred, rage, and a burning desire to eradicate those who you feel are beneath you."

"N-no... no, I'm not." Eric was shaking, his heartbeat quickened.

"You enjoy it, don't you? The feeling you get every time you strike down a foe. The moment in which the life of your enemies draws to a close, right before your very eyes. Yes, that is why you became a so-called 'protector.' And the wealth and fame, I can only imagine the ecstasy behind such spoils."

"I said can it!" Eric shouted as he ran towards Hunhau, ready to pack a wallop on the skeleton's face. Suddenly, Uacmitun Ahau sprung out of the crater and charged towards the azure knight. The spectral creature slammed into the mech with enough force to shove it away from him and his partner in crime.

After getting back up, he heard his teacher once more.

"Eric, don't let him get to you. He's only trying to bait you."

"I-is what he's saying true?" Eric grunted as he tried to recover from that last attack.

"Wha-- no! That was his thing, Eric. He played with mind games all the time, planting false thoughts when the going got too tough for him. You need to be stronger than that. That's why I chose him as your opponent. I got faith in you, Eric."

Once the pilot was back on his feet, still unsure how to process the death god's words, his enemy spoke aloud once more.

"Now, prepare to witness what no mortal has ever seen!"

Both Hunhau and Uacmitun Ahau's auras grew around them, the feathered brother screeching as if it was proclaiming an early victory. The green flames and black smoke began to entangle.

"Here is a secret only a few gods are aware of. When we first came to this life-giving planet my brother and I originally existed as one singular being. Naturally, in order to become the god of gods, I needed a right-hand man. And what better person to trust than yourself? So, I had split my power in half, resulting in the two entities you see before you! However, you have pushed us to the point where we must fuse to become whole once more!"

The two auras were completely intertwined and started swirling around the pair in a dark cyclone. Eric was too frightened to even understand what was going on. Both Hunhau and Uacmitun Ahau disappeared in the whirlwind of energy until the cyclone collapsed in on itself. The climax created a bright flash of emerald light and a shockwave that stunned Eric.

Dust clouds blinded his vision along with the inferno and ash from the wildfire. Suddenly, the skies darkened as pitch-black clouds gathered from all directions.

"I always preferred to work in the dark," whispered a deep voice, unrecognizable to Eric. It sounded nothing like either of the two gods from before.

He managed to catch a tall, thin silhouette before it raised its hand and swung, clearing the air of the dust. Standing before him was neither Hunhau nor Uacmitun Ahau. Instead, it was a larger being similar to the skeletal god, a full head taller than Draco Azul in fact. Only its bones were now covered in a layer of dried, shriveled, leathery skin. Yet, its face still resembled that of a skull, with bare teeth, no nose, and empty glowing eye sockets. This new enemy wore a hooded cloak much like the bird's that draped over its chest, back, and shoulders. Around its waist was an elongated skirt that barely touched the ground and obscured the creature's legs.

"I mentioned before that you possessed traits of a destroyer such as myself," the new death god spoke, "yet, I know with certainty, that you are *nothing* compared to the likes of me!"

Eric remained petrified by the chilling tone of his foe's voice as he slowly approached the mech.

"You lack the resolve to embrace your true potential, a mistake I aim to *never* repeat! Behold, your true opponent: *Cizin!*"

The mere bellowing of the god was enough to shake the very ground they stood on. Draco Azul lost its balance and fell on one knee.

"Yes, do bow down to your superior, False Idol, and prepare to spend an eternity of torture."

Cizin summoned the Dark Flames to form a massive burning spiked club in his right hand, along with black smoke to create a smoldering shield in the other.

"Any last words before I end your time within this mortal realm?"

Eric had heard enough of this god and grew tired of listening to his own inner voice as well. The thoughts of weakness and failure were there long before they were uttered by the demonic entity. He did not wish to hear them any longer. And so, as the god's confidence grew, so had the pilot's anger. Not towards his foe, but towards himself. In his mind, he believed that if he wished to purge himself of these thoughts, he had to smite the devilish monster that stood before him.

"Yeah," Eric proclaimed as he stood back up. "Draco Fang!"

The Primal Warrior's right blade shot from its forearm and landed perfectly in the mech's hand. Cizin raised his club and threw down his weapon at his smaller opponent. At the last second, Draco Azul wrapped his scarf around his blade and held it with both hands at the falling armament. The weapons clashed, and to Cizin's shock, the Dark Flames were still no match against the scarf, which was now protecting the blade from certain destruction. It did, however, contain enough power to slowly push down on Draco Azul, its feet digging deep into the ground.

"Who in blazes created your infernal contraption?" Cizin shouted before he raised his club in preparation for another swing.

Draco Azul dodged just in time. Eric realized that due to Cizin's increased size, his speed had been slightly reduced. It was the break he needed to counter with an attack of his own.

"Draco Striker!"

The proceeding beam of lightning was half the strength of the one Eric used against Hunhau and Uacmitun Ahau, but it was enough to destroy Cizin's shield. He now barely had enough energy for one more shot.

"You believe your accursed armor is enough to kill me?" Cizin was no longer using the chilling calm voice from before. Now, he was falling prey to his own emotions.

Both warriors clashed their weapons, each blow set the Earth asunder with tremors that traveled for miles. It was not too long until Eric was beginning to feel his body reaching his limit. Though, it did not seem like Cizin was getting tired anytime soon. He knew he had to end things before the god could outlast him.

As he battled the death god's true form, he studied his opponent's movements, just as he did with Ekchuah. He found that the god was very protective of his abdomen. This must have meant that the blade was capable of piercing his skin and mortally wounding him. He just had to find a means of leaving his foe wide open. Surely, the same tactic would not work twice. Another Draco Striker blast could be blocked by his club, which would leave Draco Azul completely drained.

Suddenly, he realized that he had one more blade in his left arm. He backed away from Cizin, motivating the enraged deity to close the distance.

"Draco Fang!"

The blade launched out of Draco Azul's forearm. Simultaneously, Eric caught his second blade while throwing his first one at his undead nemesis. The weapon tore through Cizin's skirt, pinning it to the soil he stood on. Cizin stumbled and turned to look at what had halted his progress. *This is it!* thought Eric as he rushed in for the final blow. Cizin had seen the Primal Warrior charging towards him and swung his club with one hand.

Remembering Ekchuah's advice on timing, Eric had Draco Azul leap over the god's wide swing. At that moment, he noticed the deathly creature charging one last fireball with his free hand. Eric readied his scarf by having it rushed towards his adversary's free limb. The force of the cloth managed to knock his aim just enough for the fireball to graze Draco Azul's helmet.

With nothing stopping him now, Draco Azul stabbed into Cizin's chest as he landed on the god. The deity gasped in pain as the mech's weight pushed the knife down to his stomach. Liquid green blood, the culmination of all the life force he had stolen throughout his time on Earth, seeped out of his body.

"Damn you, False Idol! You cannot do this! You're not a god. Your power was given to you; mine was earned!"

"Earned?" Eric questioned his gravely injured opponent. "You've stolen the lives of countless people and you call that power '*earned*'?"

Draco Azul pulled his other blade from Cizin's skirt. With both weapons in hand, it went on to deliver slash after slash at the lord of the underworld. Every cut, every stab, every slice to the god's body resulted in further screams of agony and more blood splattered on the mech's armor. Eric was no longer strategizing, no longer thinking -- all he wanted was to make this abhorrent thing suffer.

After a minute of furious attacks, Eric's depleting strength forced him to stop. The god that once claimed to become the next god-king had lost all his strength. His Dark Flame had been extinguished, and nearly all his life-giving blood had been poured onto the ground and across his opponent's body. The ethereal creature fell on his back with the last of his strength slowly drifting away.

As Eric panted, he heard a faint chuckle. A chuckle that grew into a maniacal laugh. He walked over to his defeated foe.

"What the hell?"

"Ha! It appears you've proven me wrong, Metal Idol. You *do* have the resolve to become a destroyer, a *true* God of Death."

The god spent his last moments laughing, with each chuckle boiling Eric's blood. The last thing he wanted was the respect of such a vile being.

"Damn you! Draco Wing!"

Eric screamed as he flew once more into the sky. He gathered the remaining energy he had left into Draco Azul's right foot and rained down one final attack to bring an end to the death god's reign.

"Draco Kick!"

The moment Draco Azul's lightning charged kick landed, Cizin's body completely evaporated along with the burnt remains of the jungle. Draco Azul had gone well beyond its limits and began to break down following the attack. Eric felt immeasurable pain in all his joints. He closed his eyes as his robot's vision shut down. He huddled to the ground until suddenly, the sensation was gone. Eric opened his eyes to find that he was back in the serene blue void.

Standing before him was a simulated version of his coach Ekchuah. "Eric, do you know what you just did?" the AI asked in a stern yet worried manner.

"I... killed Cizin, right?"

"Kid, you wiped out the last of the merchants along with destroying any chance of the Maya traveling up and down the routes ever again!"

"I-I didn't know. I thought... I just wanted to make sure that bastard was dead."

"Well, you certainly did a fine job, and at the cost of sacrificing everything that Draco Azul stands for."

"What? Giving mercy to scum like Cizin?"

"To preserve the innocent, Eric! To protect those who can't protect themselves."

Eric was quiet for a few seconds. In a pathetic attempt to excuse his irresponsible actions, he uttered the only thing he could think of.

"W-well I don't see what the big deal is. It's just a simulation anyway. It's not like any of this is real."

"Just a simulation, huh?" Whatever feeling of empathy Ekchuah carried in his voice was no longer present. "Gee, I never thought of it that way. I guess it's ok if we let everyone die in these practice sessions, huh? Why focus on minimizing collateral damage? That don't mean squat unless we kill the bad guys good. That's what *really* matters, right?"

At that moment, Eric realized just how incredibly stupid he was.

"L-look Ekchuah, I didn't mean--"

Ekchuah cut him off with a raised a finger. "Exactly! In fact, I'm gonna give you one more mission. You're gonna see the extent our enemies can go to when they don't give a *damn* about anyone but themselves. The kind of beings we're meant to be better than."

Ekchuah's avatar disappeared and the virtual world transformed into a scene right out of Dante's Inferno. Surrounding Draco Azul, now back to peak physical condition, were enormous pyramids, platforms, statues, and all other manners of stone structures. Yet, the beauty of these man-made achievements was obscured in utter pandemonium and destruction.

Everywhere Eric looked he saw the plant and soil-based houses set ablaze by lightning that almost seemed to be intentionally aimed by some unseen force. More and more bolts flew down from the heavens onto the hellscape. Eric covered his head but quickly noticed that the bolts were avoiding him and instead targeting every other structure in the vicinity.

Numerous city dwellers ran from their crumbling abodes in the hopes of escaping their peril, only for most to be stricken down by the lightning storm. The few that avoided the horrific storm ran past the burnt corpses of their families, friends, and neighbors in desperation. Eric panicked. He did not know where to even begin. He glanced up into the sky, desperately looking for the source of the abnormal storm. Then, his enhanced hearing continued to focus on the horrific screams of men, women, and children alike. He turned around to see the fleeing people and ran over to them, shielding a large crowd by absorbing the lightning as they ran.

As they neared the city's exit, the storm suddenly halted. The only thing that could be heard were the cries of the natives and the crackling of cinder. Eric looked in all directions for what could be causing this terrifying phenomenon. Still, he saw nothing. Then, it began to rain.

As the downpour increased, so too did the heavy gale. Eric was now struggling to stand. He tried to stay low to the ground and position Draco Azul in a way that would protect everyone from this new threat. Yet, he saw many innocent lives swept away in the cyclone. Every life that whizzed past Draco Azul's mechanical eyes brought a tear to Eric's face. The massive crowd he protected had now dwindled to a mere fraction consisting of orphaned children, widowed spouses, and broken elders.

Just as Eric was about to use his scarf to wrap around the survivors, a gargantuan object drove itself into Draco Azul's body, knocking him into a nearby pyramid. Eric attempted to recover from the double impact and remove himself from the rubble. He turned to the people but found that he was too late. The cylindrical-shaped object that charged him appeared to be consuming the last of the survivors.

It had a long serpentine body, covered head to tail in green feathers. Its limbs appeared to be folded wings and its gaping maw was covered in blood. It raised its body and spread out its wings. The massive figure towered over the Primal Warrior. The monstrosity howled into the clouds with a shriek so high pitch that the pilot's eardrums felt like they were about to burst. What was this creature? A god? A Diablo?

Quickly, a memory came to him, a memory from his time in college. Each civilization within Latin America spoke of a terrifying creature, a feathered serpent that could command the storms and held a high rank among the gods. It went by many names, yet its Aztec moniker remained the most prevalent in modern times: Quetzalcoatl.

Out of sheer panic, Eric unleashed all his energy into Draco Azul's strongest attack, the Draco Striker. The blast hit the feathered serpent at point-blank range. Yet, the storm god stood there, seemingly unaffected by the attack. Eric's body trembled, his heart was beating furiously, and his mind raced for any sort of plan to defeat this beast.

All the while, the god stared at the mech. Eric could tell that it was not looking at the robot. No, it was leering straight at him. Its eyes were unlike any snake he had ever witnessed. They were almost human. Within those eyes, he saw malevolence, apathy, disgust, and most of all, fury.

The god-beast lunged at Draco Azul with such speed that Eric had no time to react. The feathered serpent clamped its jaws over the mech's head and thrashed his body around, breaking each of the robot's limbs and bashing it against the pyramid it previously laid in.

Quetzalcoatl threw the azure knight to the ground and slowly wrapped around its limp body. Eric could not help but scream and cry as he saw the monstrous deity squeeze his body to within an inch of his life.

Just as when the serpent was about to lay the killing strike, the entire simulation shut down, the beast disappearing as it was mere meters away from Draco Azul's broken head.

At this point, everything went dark. Eric, still reeling from the experience, forced his still shaking hands to take off the helmet.

He looked around to see Ekchuah, standing there with a look of sorrow and regret.

"Eric. Look… I, uh, I realize what I did. I shouldn't have done that."

The young man looked at his visor and gently laid it on the floor before sitting down next to it. His legs were completely sore. He sat there rewinding the events that led up to his confrontation with the legendary Quetzalcoatl.

"You have every right to be upset. I was wrong to make you experience one of the worst days of my life," the AI coach tried to explain.

His pupil turned to him. "No, I…"

Eric held no anger, hate, or any venomous emotion towards the AI for such trauma. Somehow, deep down in his shaken soul, he felt he deserved it.

"I needed to see that," Eric muttered as he struggled to get back up, though his weathered muscles refused to budge from their resting spot. Upon seeing his student struggle, Ekchuah sat down beside him.

"That memory you just saw was the fate of Teotihuacan, the largest Mesoamerican city in all of Mexico's history… and the location of our final confrontation with the gods."

"What happened?"

"Their king, the one you know as Quetzalcoatl, challenged us after a few more skirmishes with the lower tier gods. We managed to win, but my partner's body was too broken to carry on afterward… and the entire city was lost."

That's right! Eric realized as he remembered that to this day, modern archeologists still had no idea what happened to Teotihuacan and its people. If only they knew the true horrors that took place.

"If I'm to keep Mexico and the rest of the world safe, I can't be anything like those gods."

"Well, they ain't all bad. I just happened to show you the worst of the bunch."

Upon hearing those words, Eric had to confess. "Lately, I find myself losing control of myself. Like I can't hold back. Those things Cizin said… I think they're true."

"Listen, Eric!" Ekchuah sternly ordered. "I've known you long enough to know you're nothing like them. You've got a heart, and I've seen you use it every time we're out there in the field. You just gotta keep a level head on your shoulders and remember the mission. Don't worry, kid. I got your back."

Eric listened to his concerned coach. His words did set him mostly at ease, yet there was still that lingering doubt in the back of his head. The thought that he could easily lose himself in the heat of the moment. Of course, he knew the mission. He knew he was fighting for the people of Earth. Yet, the longer he kept away from them, the further and further that world felt to him, making the mission all the more difficult to uphold.

He could barely remember what life was like before Draco Azul, what it felt like to have a meaningful human connection. He was already living an isolated life before, barely any family and no real friends. Crusading alongside Draco Azul and Ekchuah has only served to sever his ties even further. He thought of the Rodriguez family from Ensenada and how his reckless actions got them killed. As much as he might yearn to interact with the outside world, he feared he would only cause more death and destruction. For a moment, he thought he was becoming more of a threat than the Diablos themselves.

Then he reminisced about the people he rescued in Mexico City, Ensenada, Guanajuato, and many more locations. He remembered that there were countless people like the Rodrigueze's whose lives were depending on him and him alone. At that moment, he was determined to try his damnedest to keep the raging beast within him from hurting anyone else.

He immediately buried these thoughts to the recesses of his mind and looked over at Ekchuah. He noticed that his only friend was still bothered by the state he was in. He forced a smile and tried to keep his AI companion from worrying any further.

"Thanks, coach. I needed that."

Ekchuah smiled in return. "Good. By the way, the rain ended a while ago and the sun's gonna rise in an hour. Best we get moving before the early morning tourists arrive."

Eric slowly got up but was still too tired to stand for long.

"Don't worry, I'll take over while you rest. Just let me know where to go."

The young pilot thought about his present location. He knew they were currently situated near the northernmost point of the Mexican southern border and had inspected the entire Yucatán Peninsula.

"Let's try heading south. I don't think we've gone there yet."

"Know any decent places there, buddy?" Ekchuah asked.

"I'll let you decide," Eric replied as he started walking to the cockpit's back room.

Ekchuah opened a holographic window of a map of Mexico. He zoomed in on the southernmost state of Mexico. He opened several more windows of various locations until one happened to catch his attention.

"How about Chiapas? We could hide out in the mountains there."

Eric stopped by the door and looked toward Ekchuah.

"Sounds good to me, coach."

Eric smiled one last time before retiring to his quarters.

END

DRACO AZUL: LEGACY OF VALOR

The moonlight shined over the wide canyons and mountainous valleys that cover the Mexican state of Chiapas. Within this wide stretch of highlands, a gargantuan bird-like shadow swiftly glided over the rugged terrain with ease. Such a sight would be greatly disturbing for any of the locals still awake. However, a look up at the sky would be enough to calm their nerves, for the owner of the massive silhouette was Draco Azul, Mexico's great defender.

In an effort to scope out potential danger, the giant robot had been moving across the country, all due in part to the mech's pilot, Eric Martinez, and his trusty AI mentor, Ekchuah. The duo made it a priority to fly at night to avoid causing any disturbances as they surveyed each area for suspicious activity. After a week of covering the lower half of the county, their search yielded no results. However, to Eric, it was a far better alternative to sitting around doing nothing.

As their midnight investigation ended, the humanoid machine retreated into Sumidero Canyon. There, Eric slept well into the afternoon as his teacher stood guard. The pair had become well used to keeping away from the public spotlight, with Ekchuah providing his pupil the proper time to rest and train in between his duties as the Primal Warrior's pilot.

Yet, as the days passed, Ekchuah noticed his protégé falling into a slump. He spoke less, slept irregularly, made no attempt to reach out to the outside world, and was seemingly distracted whenever the two of them sparred. It appeared as if his role as the world's savior was weighing heavily on him and had started to take its toll. Though he would never in a million years admit this to Ekchuah, the AI could tell that he was burying these doubts as much as he could and that they were eating his fighting spirit from the inside out.

This conflict within his student's heart also resulted in a darker side of Eric emerging. Back when he introduced Eric to virtual reality training, the artificial instructor noticed a berserk nature emerging as he fought his electronically simulated opponents. With overt brutality, he would take all his anger and frustration out on his foes. This behavior would repeat upon future training sessions, but never with Ekchuah himself. During the duo's one-on-one sparring matches Ekchuah could tell Eric was pulling his punches, almost afraid to hurt his coach despite him being unable to feel pain. Ekchuah knew that he had to reach out to the struggling hero in some way, for both his sake and the world's.

By midday, Eric exited his resting quarters, ready to begin another day's worth of training. Yet rather than being greeted by the sight of his only friend, he instead encountered a hologram of a young boy in the middle of the cockpit. He was taken aback by its presence as he was used to Ekchuah being the only holographic entity within Draco Azul. He slowly approached the figure, which did not move at all and had a blank stare. He appeared to be a teenager, perhaps a good ten years younger than Eric, with bronze-toned skin and long black hair. Given his wardrobe, which consisted of little more than a loincloth, armbands, a necklace, and sandals, Eric presumed he was from the Maya civilization, having seen it firsthand through Ekchuah's simulations.

While inspecting the hologram from head to toe, a small detail immediately caught his attention. The teenager was wearing a device on his left wrist identical to the DraCom he wore. This device was used to keep in contact with Ekchuah and Draco Azul whenever he was outside the cockpit. *Who is this kid*, Eric thought, *and what's his relationship to Draco?*

"Put it together yet?" a voice behind him said.

"Gah! Warn me next time, would ya? Geez," Eric loudly responded.

He turned to find that it was Ekchuah's hologram form, taking shape right before him. Eric then turned back to take one more look at the teen before it hit him.

"Was he... Draco's pilot?" he asked as he pointed at the figure.

"Not just any pilot -- the very *first* pilot! Way back in 275 AD at the tender age of fifteen. His name: Yochi, the Child of Hope."

Eric had known there were numerous pilots before him during the height of the Maya civilization but had never actually seen any of them. The closest he got was through experiencing VR missions that were based on their numerous exploits.

"He's so young," was all Eric could say as he attempted to process what it must have been like for a child his age to be the first human ever to wield the power of Draco Azul.

"Kids back then grew up pretty fast," replied his holographic coach. "At fifteen, you were already considered an adult and believe me, *this* kid went through a lot to prepare himself. Ten years, in fact. Yet, no amount of training could ever prepare him for what life had in store."

"Jesus. No pressure, huh? How long did he last?"

"Now, now. Let's not get too ahead of ourselves," Ekchuah said with a smile.

With a wave of his arms, the hologram of Yochi dissolved and in its place was an expansive map that took up the whole room. Eric had to step back to view the entire projection. With another gesture of his hand, Ekchuah activated a seat behind Eric. Once it sprung forth from the floor, the young man sat down and watched the holographic light show take place.

It was then he recognized the area as the ancient Maya city of Calakmul. In the center was Draco Azul surrounded by a massive crowd. However, this version of the blue giant did not wear a scarf, but rather a massive regal cape that draped over its shoulders.

In his early days of piloting the mech, Eric had seen archived images of the robot in its early years and realized it must have lost its cape at some point in time. Despite his curiosity, he was often so busy fighting and training that he always forgot to ask Ekchuah how exactly this accessory was lost. Did it deteriorate over time, or all at once by some powerful foe? Could it have been Quetzalcoatl?

Above the map was a massive mechanical object that eclipsed the entire city. As the cylindrical craft lifted itself up, Ekchuah proceeded to regale the wide-eyed pilot with the events that took place centuries prior.

"The year was 250 AD. The aliens you designated as 'Samaritans' had just finished constructing their gift for mankind, Draco Azul -- or, *Ya'axkan* as he was called back then."

The hologram then shifted once more into the form of an adult man in his 20s in Draco Azul's pilot suit. The man looked vaguely similar to Yochi, with much shorter hair and a stockier build. He looked incredibly uncomfortable in his technological surroundings.

"Initially, the Samaritans chose the high priest that ruled over Calakmul, one of the Maya's oldest cities, as Draco's pilot. However, the immense amount of power at his disposal was too much for him to bear and the technology was well beyond his understanding."

Again, the display changed to showcase the high priest looking upward at the Primal Warrior, sitting on the ground in a slouched posture. In the man's arms was an infant.

"Not wanting to let this incredible gift go to waste, the high priest decided that his firstborn son, Yochi, would be Draco Azul's proper pilot. He hadn't even turn one yet, but his father thought it was best for the pilot to be someone who would be raised with Draco Azul and its remarkable tech. That's where I came in."

From there, Eric viewed the scene shift into a young, five-year-old Yochi sparring with a humanoid hologram. Its body was devoid of any clothes, accessories, or any anatomical details save for a face, fingers, toes, and an average muscular build.

"Hold on, *that's* you?"

"Yes, that's me," Ekchuah said with an embarrassed tone. "The Samaritans never gave me a proper look back then. Instead, my form was based on the average appearance of a male human."

"How'd you get the look you have today?"

"Look, this isn't about me alright?" Ekchuah annoyingly replied. "Once he turned five, I started showing Yochi the ropes as he got ready to helm the reins of Draco. By 275 AD, his journey would finally start…"

Ekchuah then waved his hand, causing a number of scenes to take place in front of Eric as if he was watching a 3D movie. His mentor walked over to where he sat and the two began to watch the past unfold before their very eyes, recorded eons ago, recreated and translated for the present day.

***

The cockpit to the metal giant known as Ya'axkan opened its doors and allowed Yochi to enter its cockpit. The warm sunset light gleaming behind him illuminated the dark empty room before its electronically powered devices lit up the corridor. Yochi looked behind him where he saw his father, his family, and the rest of his city loudly cheering for his success as the controller of the mechanical titan.

For the last fifteen years, word of a colossal warrior with skin a thousand times stronger than obsidian and taller than the largest pyramids laid in slumber within Calakmul. It was said that it was a gift delivered not by gods, but by strangers from the stars to serve as the Maya's protector. For over a decade it lay in slumber among the city's temples and shrines. Many outsiders believed it was simply biding its time, waiting for a worthy challenger.

Yet little did the people outside of the city know that the warrior did not act on its own accord, but was meant to be controlled by human thoughts and actions. As the high priest's eldest son, Yochi was meant to answer the call to protect his people from forces too great for mankind to handle alone. Since he was a child he studied under his master, Ekchuah, a being of pure light. Each day he would rigorously improve his ability to utilize each of Ya'axkan's talents, readying himself for the day he would start his journey. That day was finally upon him.

Days ago, villagers from the city of Tikal had visited their land for assistance. They reported that their neighboring cities were attacked by subterranean demons, consuming their people and livestock at night. For fear that their city would be next, they had asked for the help of Ya'axkan to smite the demons for good. Plenty of people had previously traveled to Calakmul, praying and begging for the colossus to destroy their enemies. Yet, their selfish calls went unanswered. However, in the case of the nightmares from deep beneath the Earth, both Ekchuah and the high priest believed the time was right for Yochi to begin his crusade.

The doors to the cockpit closed before Yochi. The adolescent wondered if this would be the last time, he would ever see his home, his friends, and his family. His heart raced and his breathing grew heavy as doubts plagued his mind. Just then, his teacher materialized before him.

"Hey, hey, what's the problem? You getting cold feet?" the ghostly apparition asked.

"I'm sorry, Master. It's nothing," the boy responded.

"I heard your heartbeat. That certainly doesn't sound like nothing."

The boy turned to face his mentor as he attempted to put on a brave face.

"I'm just excited! Now, let's get started then," Yochi proclaimed with a cocky attitude. "Can't keep those people waiting, right?"

This demeanor was present during most of his training sessions with Ekchuah; as far as he knew, he was the best combatant in his village. He grew comfortable with his place at the top. Of course, being the son of a high priest afforded him only the best lifestyle one could receive. One such luxury was the avoidance of any real combat. This was a luxury that he quickly took for granted throughout his life. Now, it was time for him to put his skills to the ultimate test.

"Kid, I can see right through you as much as you can see through me."

The smile on the boy faded.

"Look, it's natural that you're feeling the jitters. Heck, I would be too. But it's gonna be alright. I got your back."

Silence fell upon the teenager. "Hmph, nothing gets past you." The boy smiled as his nerves began to calm down.

"Damn right, kid! Now get ready, time's a-wastin'!"

Yochi stepped onto the center of the room. There, millions of nanomachines wrapped around his body, covering every square inch of his being save for his head. He had worn this suit multiple times during his simulations. The boy still found the suit uncomfortably tight, yet oddly flexible.

"Alright, Master. I'm ready."

Multiple mechanical appendages lowered from the ceiling to attach the arm, leg, and chest attachments that synched his body to that of his gigantic avatar. Finally, the visor lowered and fitted itself onto his eyes, but not before the nanotech suit stretched to cover his entire scalp, ears, and eyes.

His vision was completely obscured before his visor activated as the blue titan's eyes began scanning the terrain. Outside, Ya'axkan's entire body slowly stood up. Its head raised high into the air as the crowd cheered below.

Yochi turned his head, as did the giant. He looked down at the people on the ground, appearing to be little more than ants from his new perspective. Once more his heartbeat quickened -- this time not due to fear, but exhilaration. He waved his hand at this family, and so too did Ya'axkan. His arm felt a lot heavier as a reflection of the metal giant's immense weight. While he had felt this sensation through simulations, finally experiencing it all in real life was the thrill of a lifetime.

"Wow, this is unreal!"

"Be careful, kid. Don't want to step on anyone now," Yochi heard from his right.

"Got it, Master!"

He gestured for the crowd to move aside with his arms. Once everyone was at a safe distance from the behemoth, Ya'axkan took its first steps out of the city and into the jungle. Yochi felt the vibrations from every step he took as he flattened numerous trees with ease.

"Should I activate the wings?" the young pilot asked.

"Nah, not yet. I don't think you're quite ready yet."

"Not ready? Don't you think I practiced enough?"

"Not in real life you haven't. You gotta walk before you can fly."

Yochi rolled his eyes and continued to march forward towards Tikal.

***

Over the next few hours, the metal giant strode across the land, passing by several villages along the way. As the behemoth passed each settlement, numerous villagers were left gasping at the striking visage of their guardian. For the last decade and a half, they had all heard tall tales and rumors of the titanic warrior from the stars. For some, they had seen it with their own eyes in Calakmul but were now shocked to see the towering figure in motion.

The more people Yochi encountered the closer he examined each and every one of their appearances. Not to bask in their admiration, but to remember their faces. To remember that these individuals were now under his protection. On top of surveying the people, Yochi's electronic companion advised him to keep track of the scenery.

The adolescent had previously explored the neighboring cities and locations around his hometown, but never ventured beyond the safety of his land. Now, encased in a gargantuan suit of armor, he no longer needed to fear for his life, at least not from the common dangers known to his people.

As Ya'axkan arrived at the great city of Tikal in the late afternoon, a celebration awaited it. People from the entire city welcomed their savior and offered numerous gifts: from corn, beans, and potatoes to clothing, jewelry, and pottery.

"Quite the welcome wagon they brought us," Ekchuah commented.

"Boy, I'll say," his student responded.

"Too bad you won't be enjoying any of it."

"What? Ah, come on, Master. That ain't fair!"

"Look, kid. If you wanna keep your friends and family safe, you'll keep your identity a secret. As far as everyone knows, Ya'axkan has got a mind of his own."

Frustrated over not being able to reap the benefits of his newfound role, Yochi could not help but turn away from his mentor and pout.

"Besides, we can't have you celebrating just yet. Ya gotta *earn* it first! Once this is all over, *then* you can party back home."

Yochi felt Ekchuah place his hand on his shoulder.

"I guarantee it."

The teenager smiled and decided to follow his advisor's instructions. Ya'axkan walked around the city until it was positioned near the settlement's largest temple and a neighboring acropolis on the outskirts of the city. Every half hour, Yochi relocated Ya'axkan to a different spot around Tikal, circling the entire 222 square mile area until the sun retired into the horizon and the locals retreated to their homes. In between Yochi's rotations, he kept vigil over the city, its inhabitants, and the surrounding area, memorizing every inch of the land. Ekchuah also made it a point to test Yochi's knowledge of all of Ya'axkan's functions, from the machine's lightning-based attacks to the multiple uses of its blades and cape.

***

Deep into the night, Yochi continued to stand guard over Tikal. His master had already offered him bizarre supplements and nourishments to keep him energized. Nervous over the possibility of becoming distracted, he kept small talk with Ekchuah to an absolute zero. Ekchuah could detect the discomfort his pupil was experiencing and gave him the space he needed while also providing him a second pair of observant eyes.

By the time the moon had reached the midpoint of its journey across the starry canvas, Yochi started feeling light tremors beneath Ya'axkan's feet.

"I'm sure you caught that, kid," Ekcuach commented.

"Y-yeah, what do I do?"

"What do you think you should do?"

"Uh… get ready to engage in combat?" asked Yochi, just as he felt another tremor.

"You could do that, but wouldn't you rather keep whatever's coming away from the city?"

"Right. How about we track where it's coming from?"

"Attaboy!" Ekchuah opened an application within Yochi's visor, allowing him to view a map of the area with a section glowing red, located several miles right from where Ya'axkan stood. "Whatever's making that racket is located here. Get ready to move out."

Yochi remembered his years of training, the countless hours he spent preparing for this moment. With his determination at an all-time high, he set out to locate and exterminate the mysterious threat.

Ya'axkan marched forward through the jungles, shaking the earth with each massive step. Yochi kept track of the map visible within his field of vision. The tremors grew more frequent and stronger the closer the metal warrior got to the epicenter.

Suddenly the ground beneath Ya'axkan collapsed, causing the giant to tumble into a massive pit. The warrior's blue and white armor was buried under enough soil to shape into a large hill.

"What the hell was that?" Yochi asked.

"Could've been a trap," Ekchuah replied.

Yochi used this moment as an opportunity to bring Ya'axkan's mighty cape to life. He concentrated his thoughts on the otherworldly cloth and imagined it lifting into the air. On command, the cloak widened itself and hurled the mounds of dirt in all directions. Freed from his earth-based prison, Yochi scanned the entire area. All around him, he looked upon a series of large holes along the walls of the crater he found himself in.

"Or," Ekchuah pondered, "this could've been the habitat of some subterranean creature."

"Whatever it was, it must've dug through the ground multiple times," the pilot added, to which the artificial intelligence agreed.

"Most likely. By making the foundation of the ground unstable, Ya'axkan's weight alone was enough to break it."

From the corner of his eye, Yochi spotted a pair of glowing red eyes within one of the tunnels.

"Master! I found our foe!" he shouted before getting into his battle stance. Just then, more pairs of eyes appeared within the surrounding burrows. "Or should I say 'foes?'"

The initial glaring eyes moved towards the tunnel's entrance, revealing itself in the moonlight. It was an animal, unlike anything Yochi had ever seen. At thirty meters long, it was half the size of Ya'axkan. The growling beast walked on four paws and featured pale hairless skin, a thin bony tail, long spines along its back, large ears, and massive fangs. Its appearance resembled an absurd blend of a rodent and a canine.

More of the beast's brood followed suit. Soon, Yochi had ten enemies ready to pounce at the giant guardian at any time.

"Damn, what do we do, Master?"

"Let's get out of this pit first and even the battlefield."

"Got it. Kaaan Flight!"

Massive wings sprouted from the machine's back. With one massive leap, Ya'axkan flew into the sky, just as the pack of underground horrors leaped at where it once stood.

Yochi's heart pounded as he felt the surge of adrenaline flowing through his veins. Through Ekchuah's guidance, he found the perfect spot and landed on solid ground feet first.

The young pilot turned back towards the pit and witnessed the animals climbing out of it and rushing at him. One by one each monstrosity pounced at the azure fighter, only to be knocked out with a single punch, or thrown to the side. Yochi was thankful that his opponents were weak enough to overpower. However, what they lacked in strength, they made up in sheer numbers.

As Yochi and Ya'axkan fought back against the hellish fiends, Ekchuah observed the earlier foes his pupil knocked out regaining consciousness and joining the fight. That was when he noticed that for whatever reason, Yochi was not slaying his enemies. He would slam his fists into their faces, stomp them into the ground, and even throw their bodies against each other. Still, no matter how often they came at him, he would never take their lives. At that moment, Ekchuah realized that his student needed to learn the ultimate burden that all soldiers must carry.

"Yochi, let's retreat."

"Are you kidding me? We can't leave now!" Yochi protested.

"We are if you're not going to properly fight your enemies! If you want to keep Tikal and the rest of your people safe, you're gonna need to put an end to these guys *permanently*!"

With the pilot distracted and conflicted towards his mentor's words, four of the pale monsters jumped on Ya'axkan, pinning the mech facedown. Yochi focused once more on his avatar's massive cloth. The cape sprung forth to life and stretched itself to a length that allowed it to envelope every one of the beasts. Yochi struggled to maintain his concentration while the demons pierced their claws and teeth into Ya'axkan's armor, inflicting pain onto the pilot in the process.

"Don't lose focus, kid. You got this!" Ekchuah shouted.

Through sheer will, Yochi manipulated his cape into pulling his foes off him. Slowly, but surely, Ya'axkan got back on its feet as its cloak held each beast off the ground.

"Now strike while the iron's hot!"

Understanding Ekchuah's words, Yochi no longer hesitated and stabbed each foe with the razor-sharp blades that adorn each forearm. One stab was all it took to end each behemoth's life. Once all four were dead, Yochi had his cape release their corpses.

"Great job! But don't relax just yet."

Indeed, it was not the time to declare victory as the remaining devils of the earth got back up, only to see their deceased brethren laying before them. One of the ghostly brutes leapt into the pit as the other five ran toward Ya'axkan. Yochi, still reeling from the toll his concentration took on his physical and mental well being, forced himself to engage in combat once more. This time, he was holding nothing back.

The first of the underground beasts lunged itself at the guardian, only for its head to be pierced by one of the giant's blades.

Two more creatures came at opposite sides. At the last moment, Ya'axkan jumped out of the way as the monsters crashed into each other. With the creatures dazed from the collision, the titan grabbed both of their faces and smashed them into the ground, crushing their skulls instantly.

"There's one right on your tail!" Ekchuah warned as yet another beast attempted to ambush the metal warrior.

Quick to react, Yochi had Ya'axkan's cape lash out at the creature and throw it at the remaining foe. The last of the creatures dodged the makeshift projectile as it fell into the rocky crater, breaking its spine upon impact. Unlike the others, the final demon did not attack the blade-wielding fighter. Instead, it had remained in the background, watching the entire fight unfold. Yochi watched as the last of the underground demons paced around Ya'axkan as if it were studying the machine, waiting for the perfect opportunity to strike.

"There's no doubt about it," Yochi concluded, "this one's been waiting for a one-on-one showdown."

"Good, then let's give him one."

Deciding to switch things up, Yochi shouted out a second activation code.

"Kaaan Blade!"

Upon reciting his vocal command, Ya'axkan's right blade flew off its forearm and landed in its hand. Holding his handheld weapon out while guarding his torso with his bladed left arm, Yochi stood his ground and watched the creature's every movement. It was no longer walking circles around the soldier. Both opponents were now ready for their final duel.

As if both man and beast were in sync, each launched their final assaults on one another. The animal that had survived for so long beneath the earth was fast, but the otherworldly machine powered by the human spirit was faster. Its blade sliced cleanly through the beast's body and cleaved the creature in two. The fight was over as quickly as it began.

Yochi could not help but shed a tear for his enemy as he stared at its corpse.

"Hey, Yochi," his mentor called out to him. Very rarely did he use his name, and only during moments of pure sincerity did he ever do this.

"Yes, Master?"

"I know you like to put on this tough guy act, but I also know deep down inside you don't like getting anyone hurt. I can see that from the way you fought these guys. Having compassion for all life is important for someone like you. But sadly, that ain't enough. We all gotta do things we ain't proud of."

"I know," Yochi responded as he looked at the blood that stained Ya'ashkan's blade. "I understand that to protect my people I must slay my enemies. But I never knew it would be this difficult."

"Of course, it's hard. That's because of your humanity, Yochi. As a computer program, that's something I could never teach. It was best for you to learn for yourself."

Yochi eyed his slain enemies, then turned to Tikal, remembering each and every face he witnessed throughout the day.

"You're right, Master. It's what I must--"

Before he could finish his sentiment, Yochi felt a massive tremor, one greater than any he had experienced before. The ground broke apart, and from the earth sprouted a new pale demon, one far larger than the previous beasts. This creature had larger spines, stood on two legs, and dwarfed Ya'axkan. The beast howled at the starry sky as the ground continued to grow more unstable.

"There must be more of them underground. This big one must be the Alpha!" Ekchuah shouted.

Yochi was ready to escape but lost his footing as the ground beneath Ya'axkan collapsed into an even deeper chasm. The larger demon grabbed onto the mech to ensure its descent into the deepest pits of hell. This new beast dragged Ya'axkan miles below the surface before entering an open space where Yochi heard chittering and screeching from all directions. It was too dark for him to see anything. That was when he remembered one of Ya'axkan's capabilities.

"Master, can you activate the night vision?"

"You got it!"

While he could now see in the dark, he immediately wished he had not. Yochi found himself in an expansive network of caves, filled with countless demons. Before him stood their leader, standing on two limbs in a hunched-over posture. Its subordinates backed away from the two titans and formed a circle around them.

Bruised and battered, Yochi found himself in no position to fight. Plus, even if he did manage to subdue the alpha beast, he would have to contend with its entire family.

"I don't think we can take them all on. What do we do?"

"I've been trying to come up with a plan since we got here. Try to keep it occupied for the time being."

"Really? Is that the best you can do?"

"Hey, I don't see *you* coming up with any ideas!"

The Alpha went on the offense and whipped its tail at the unsuspecting mech. The goliath mammal then pounced on the downed warrior, who rolled away from the attack. After getting back up, the machine avoided getting hit by every one of the Alpha's attacks.

"I got it!" Ekchuah proclaimed. "We'll use our energy supply to destroy the whole damn place."

"You sure about that? What if we get buried along with them?"

"We'll improvise. On my signal, you'll do as I say, alright?"

With no other option, Yochi agreed. Just then, the Alpha managed to grab a hold of Ya'axkan's arms and bite into its shoulder. The intense pain made Yochi accidentally let go of his blade. He tried freeing his arms, but this only tightened the monster's grip.

"Start charging now, maximum power!" commanded Ekchuah.

Focusing on channeling his machine's fuel into Ya'axkan's horn, Yochi recited the first half of this technique's vocal command.

"Kaaaaan!"

Ya'axkan's eyes and horn illuminated in a bright blue aura that crackled with sparks of lightning bolts. Being so close to the bright surge of light, the Alpha's already sensitive eyes were instantly blinded. It screamed in agony, giving Yochi the chance to grab its head and slam its body to the floor.

Ya'axkan wrestled with the beast, its arms wrapped around the creature. The Alpha wildly clawed at the robot's armor to no avail as Yochi refused to give in to his torment. All around him, the other subterranean demons began to close in on Ya'axkan.

However, they stopped in their tracks as the illumination from the mechanical giant's horn grew brighter and brighter. They began to back away as the surge of energy reached its zenith. With one final twist, Ya'axkan snapped the Alpha's neck. Its body falls limp. After a moment of stunned silence, the demons charged with blind, vengeful fury.

"Now, aim for the supporting columns." With his signal given, Yochi shouted the final part of his command.

"Shiiiiiiiine!"

A concentrated blast of lightning-fueled energy erupted from Ya'axkan's horn and eviscerated the demons and sedimentary structures in its path. The azure warrior turned around to allow its blast to fire in all directions as the rest of the monsters tried to escape. Rubble started falling everywhere as the smaller caves and tunnels collapsed in on themselves.

"Aim at the roof and blow a hole out for our escape!"

Using the last of the built-up energy, Yochi lifted his head and aimed at the ceiling directly above him. With the last sparks of lightning now depleted from Ya'axkan's horn, Yochi grabbed a hold of his missing blade, activated his wings once more, and flew off into the artificial tunnel. As he launched into the air, he could hear the dying screams of the creatures struggling to find a means to escape. The higher he flew, the more distant their cries became until, finally, he had reached the surface.

"Now let's make sure these bastards never show up on our turf again."

"Right on it, Master!"

The mighty mech slammed its fist into the ground near the tunnel, causing the soil to break down and collapse in on itself.

With the battle finally over, Yochi sighed and fell on his back, as did Ya'axkan.

"Whew! We made it!"

"You had me worried there for a sec, but you managed to pull through. I'm proud of ya, kid!"

"Heh, it was nothing," Yochi said in a failed attempt to maintain his calm, snarky self.

"Still though," the pilot said as he thought back on what had transpired. "I feel bad that we had to do that to those creatures. I'm sure all they wanted to do was survive, just like us."

"Indeed, but neither of you can coexist without one eliminating the other. Judging by the info my creators programmed into me, that's always been the case. Not just on this planet, but everywhere. Survival of the fittest. Species come and go. And for those guys, it just might, unfortunately, be their time."

"Such is the tragedy of beasts as great as them I suppose."

"You got that right. Now, can ya stand?"

Yochi struggled as he managed to get Ya'axkan back on its feet.

"Ngh! I think so."

"Good. Now, let's head back to the city. If those critters don't show up for the next few days, we can head back home."

"Yes, Master. By the way, earlier you said we all have to do things we're not proud of."

"Right," said the AI, unsure where his protégé was going with his inquiry.

"Well, what is it that *you* have to do?"

"Oh, that's easy. It's having to deal with your lousy attitude!"

With that, the pair laughed as they made their way to Tikal to celebrate the beginning of their journey and the first of many victories to come.

***

As the simulation ended, the hologram within Draco Azul's cockpit dissolved before Eric and Ekchuah's eyes. Eric, bewildered by his predecessor's first outing, was left with many questions.

"What happened to you and Yochi after that?"

"Oh, we continued to have many more battles with what we eventually called the Kawak. What we dealt with back then was the first of many invasions by those things."

"The Kawak, huh? Where have I heard that name before?"

"Well, probably through the legends, as throughout the centuries their name became synonymous with an underground guardian of the underworld. Of course, only my pilots ever knew the truth about them. Using the Internet and mankind's newfound understanding of paleontology, I can conclude that they were an ancient species of mole-like *therapsids,* creatures long thought to be extinct. Essentially, the link between reptiles and mammals."

"I see, so these Kawak were like, evolved super-therapsids?"

"You could say that," Ekchuah said as he shrugged.

"So, did you guys get rid of them all?"

Ekchuah paused for a moment, as if unsure of how to answer. "Not *exactly.*"

"You mean they're still out there?"

"Now now, before you panic, know this. We were able to get rid of all the *big* ones. Later on, me and a descendant of his discovered a significantly smaller subspecies. These guys are about as threatening as any average wolf or mountain lion. They never attack humans, but they're a major pain in the ass when it comes to livestock. From the reports I've gathered, the locals refer to them by a different name."

As Ekchuah exposited on the fate of the Kawak, he opened several holographic windows, each one adorned with reports of large hairless, dog-like animals attacking goats and chickens around Mexico. Within each of the news stories, one name kept popping up again and again.

"El Chupacabra!" Eric said under his breath.

"Bingo! Seems ol' Yochi got his wish after all. He always felt bad about having to put down the Kawak, but they still managed to live on and eke out a living among the humans. Shame he never got to see his dream become a reality."

Eric was almost too afraid to ask about the fate of Draco Azul's very first pilot.

"W-what happened to him?"

"Oh, he continued fighting the Kawak, or Chupacabras I guess, and other ancient monsters we came across. Eventually, he grew old and later passed the torch to his son, beginning the cycle anew."

With a wave of his hand, Ekchuah morphed the hologram screens into the form of a tall and muscular adult male wearing a jaguar skin, a feathered headdress, and a short skirt around his waist. Eric instantly recognized the figure.

"That's you!"

"Heh, well, not exactly. After he passed away, his son and I decided to carry on his memory by having me take on his image, specifically him in his prime. It's an honor I've carried to this day."

Eric was shocked to discover that not only was he looking at the reconstructed visage of the forerunner who laid the groundwork for his role as Draco Azul's pilot, but also that the cocky, yet timid teen would go on to become an example for all future pilots to look towards.

"Gee," Eric exclaimed in an unsure tone, "I don't know how I can possibly measure up to him. The guy spent his whole life protecting everyone since he was a teenager. And he had a decade's head start on top of that! Me? I can barely hold my own against the Diablos without losing my mind."

"Look, Eric. Don't you start on that, ya hear?"

Eric looked up at his coach.

"I didn't choose to wear his face to make other pilots feel bad about themselves," Ekchuah said as he pointed at his visage. "I did it to remind my students that the impossible *is* possible. Yochi carried an *enormous* burden as Draco's first pilot. Despite all his bravado, he was scared as hell. He carried the same insecurities you did. Yet, he was determined to carve out his path in life, and he would've wanted that for everyone after him.

"So, ya see? You shouldn't have to concern yourself with living in his shadow. Rather, you should focus on creating your *own* path."

"How do I do that?" Eric asked.

"By being you, for starters." Ekchuah gave his pupil a warm smile as he bestowed his wisdom. "There's only one Eric Martinez, and only Eric Martinez can do what Eric Martinez does."

As he heard his mentor's words, Eric could imagine them coming out of the very same individual who started his journey in a position very similar to his own.

"Yeah, I guess you're right, Coach," Eric said as his spirit lifted.

"Of course, I'm right!" Ekchuah said with a grin. "How'd you think I was able to whip Yochi into shape?"

Eric chuckled alongside his friend and teacher.

Suddenly, an alarm rang as holographic screens popped up before them. Each screen showcased varying news reports of a new Diablo attacking Guadalajara after appearing in the middle of the city.

"Damn, it's another one of those random sprouters. And we're so far away!"

"Don't worry, we can get there in time. I've had a good amount of fuel saved up just in case this happened. Now get ready, kid. It's showtime!"

"On it, coach!" Eric said, his spirit reenergized for the challenge up ahead.

"By the way, when this is all said and done, let's head back here. It's a pretty decent hiding spot. Plus, everyone's gonna be looking for us up north.

"Sure, though shouldn't we be focused on the battle up ahead?" Eric said as he finished suiting up.

"Heh, I suppose your right." Ekchuah smiled, believing his newest pupil truly was capable of continuing Yochi's legacy.

Eric, now armed and ready, activated Draco Azul as he set forth to carve out his path in a way only he could.

END

BRAVURA: THE WANDERING SOLDIER

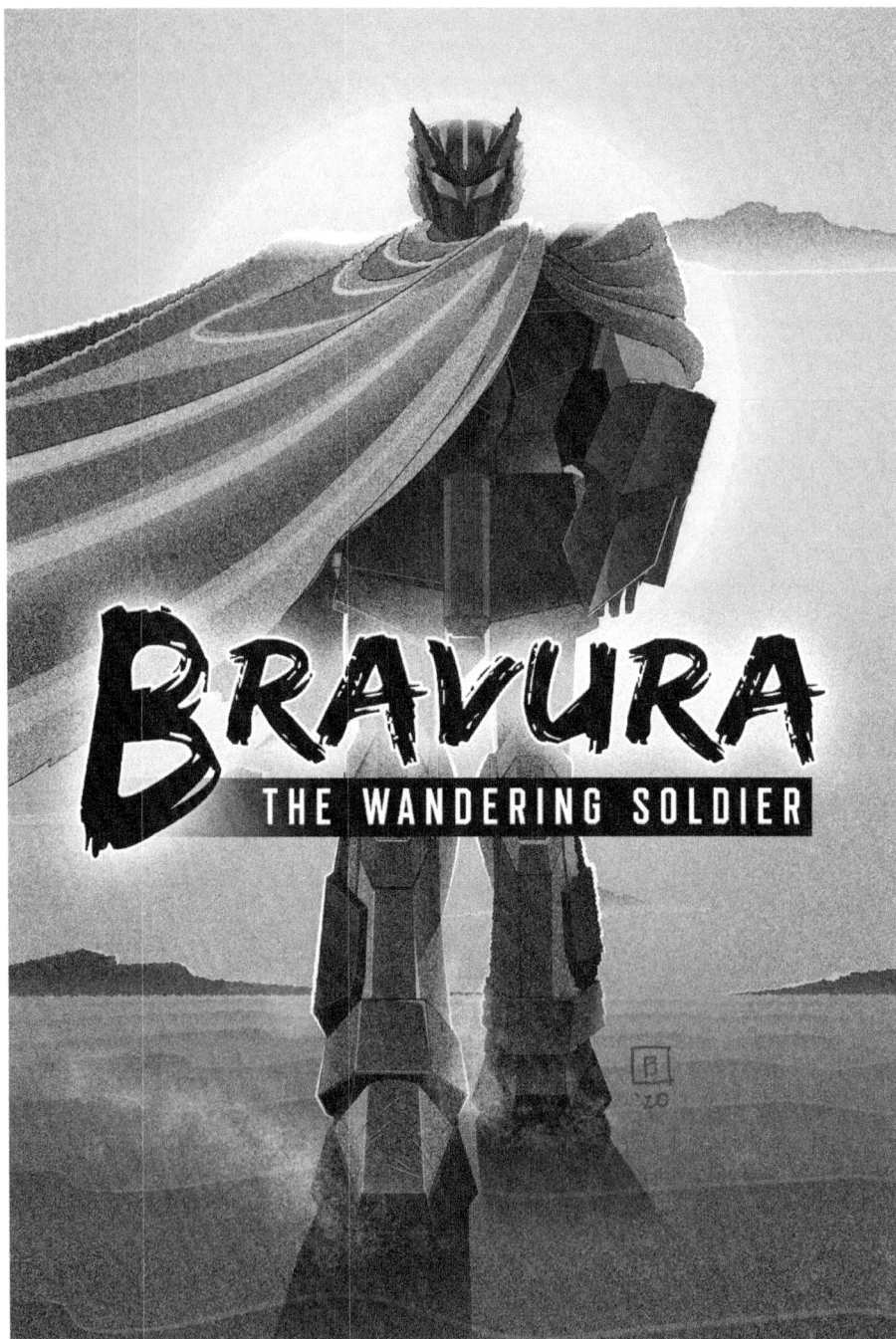

It was another blisteringly hot day in the ruins of Nevada. The radiation levels have been higher than normal, causing this summer season to be even worse than the last. On top of that, the dust storms from the east have just entered the valley. Only the strongest of the giant mutants have a chance at surviving in these harsh conditions.

Within this boiling landscape, one of the few bastions of civilization exists underneath a massive metal dome, decorated with solar panels. Its name: Nuevo Oasis. It has been said that this camp was built on the remains of one of the largest cities in what used to be the United States of America. A city that never slept, a town that was full of bright neon lights, dazzling entertainment, and gambling centers galore. Nowadays, the only legacy left of the once-bustling metropolis is the existence of a few seedy clubs where players from around the camp play their weekly poker games. As of now, it is the largest of the west side camps.

Walking towards this establishment was a single metallic figure. Standing twenty-five meters tall, it was a Colossus, the greatest of mankind's technological achievements. The machine had a humanoid frame shrouded in an elongated cloak that left only its head and legs exposed. The Colossus's head sported a wide blue visor surrounded by a dust-covered helmet and mouth plate. Keeping its visor shaded were two armored plates over each side of its forehead. The robot's legs showed off what was once pearly white and piano black armor, now covered in dirt and rust, giving it a dull yellowish-brown hue. Its armor was covered in claw, tooth, bullet, and burn marks, indicating that the mech itself had seen plenty of action from both man and mutant.

Trailing behind the Colossus was a large metal net holding the massive corpse of a bloody, fur-covered creature. The machine was pulling its dead cargo by its arm with ease. The weight of the deceased animal left a massive trench in the ground as the machine marched towards Nuevo Oasis.

At the gates stood two larger Colossi, each standing at roughly thirty meters and equipped with thick armor and large metal staffs. One of them approached their cloaked visitor. The guard piloting the machine contacted the stranger via wireless communication.

"State your business!"

The cloaked figure stood in place for a few seconds before it relayed its pilot's message to the guard's cockpit.

"I'm here to conduct a trade in exchange for rest."

"Is that so?"

The guard had his Colossus walk around the stranger's machine and examine the bag it was lugging behind. He noticed the trail of blood trickling from the enormous carcass.

"Got yourself a mutant, huh? And a mammal to boot."

"It is what it is."

"We have a process for mutant meat," the guard said before turning over to the other guard.

"Hey, Steve! We got a supplier here. Take him to the decontamination entrance."

The guard turned his mech back to the stranger.

"This place is under heavy surveillance. Make one wrong move and you're history."

The stranger gave no response. Once the second guard manipulated his Colossus into waving, signaling to follow him, the stranger had his machine do so.

The two walked around the camp for several minutes before arriving at the secondary entrance. The guard's robot inputted the password on a keypad the size of a semi-truck and the doors opened. The stranger's mech walked inside and was immediately showered like it was a giant car wash. Dirt and blood washed off the Colossus and its cargo, from which it circled down a giant drain. Though even without the dirt, the machine was still caked in an ugly brown that no amount of piping hot water could clean off.

A second set of doors opened on the other side for the stranger to walk out of. As soon as he stepped out, four Colossi, exactly like the ones that stood at the entrance, awaited him.

"We'll take your cargo and inspect it elsewhere. It's quality will determine the duration of your stay."

This has been the way business was done ever since the collapse of the economy that left every form of currency completely useless. Now, payment for one's contributions to the survival of a camp came in the form of basic necessities such as food and shelter. Those that wish to live in the camp permanently would have to contribute to its maintenance on a regular basis. The more complex the camp was, such as in Nuevo Oasis's case, the more opportunities there were. Engineers and mechanics were especially necessary.

For those that owned a Colossus, jobs that involved hunting down food, transporting resources, providing protection, and other forms of heavy labor were given the most lavish treatments. However, it all depended on how well and how long they could perform. If one were to lose their Colossus, they would be left without a job and end up forced to fend for themselves in this harsh world. The guards that worked at Nuevo Oasis were employed directly by the Council, who oversaw every single operation that kept the camp running. As long as the camp maintained their limited supply of Colossi, the guards were set for life.

With so much focus on security, Nuevo Oasis was in dire need of more freelancers. That was where the Hunter came in. He was escorted to the hangar where one other Colossus was stored. It was taller and bulkier than the Hunter's and in pristine condition, even more so than the regular guard units. The mechanics were just applying the finishing touches on its new black paint scheme, complete with a skull emblem on its chest and flaming "F" marks on each of its massive shoulder pads. It was clear to everyone that whoever owned this machine had a lot to offer the camp if the mechanics were willing to provide such accommodations for this mech.

The Hunter received a message from his escort to exit his Colossus once it was docked. Several mechanics looked up in awe at the stranger's machine. As the pilot climbed down onto a platform everyone could see what he looked like.

He wore an old, banged up aviator suit -- most likely from the War of Desolation -- only its sleeves were missing as they had been ripped off. The Hunter wore a pair of dark sunglasses that did little to hide the burn marks on the left side of his face. His leather boots and gloves did not seem to match the rest of his outfit, leaving some mechanics to assume he either lost them or traded them at some point. On the man's right shoulder, he had a tattoo that resembled a mix of the Greek symbols for alpha and omega. Lastly, he had a burlap sack tied to his belt.

As the platform lowered to the ground, the man stepped off and was greeted by the lead mechanic.

"Hey there! Name's Matt. I'm here to let you know that the package you brought got you about a week's stay here. Normally a mutant would get you just a couple days, but you brought in a rare specimen! In the meantime, my team will be responsible for your unit. You're allowed a full system's check-up and any repairs needed to keep your machine running."

Matt looked up at the soiled appearance of the Colossus in disgust.

"Unfortunately, you'll have to provide services for Nuevo Oasis for at least half a year to get any aesthetic tune-ups."

"That's fine," the Hunter said with a soft and graveled voice.

He was not looking at Matt, however. Rather, he was surveying the hangar and the other mechanics who cautiously stood before him. He then turned his attention directly at Matt.

"How long do I have to work here to get any firearms?"

"That'll cost about a couple months of service from you. Though we do have some melee weapons in storage."

The Hunter looked up at his mech and back to the local. "Nah, I got my own."

The confused mechanic looked back at the Colossus and noticed that it did not carry any weapons in its hands.

"Huh," was all Matt could say before the man walked up to him with the mysterious bag now in his hands.

"I want a private team of your best men, no questions asked. You'll say nothing to anyone about Bravura."

The mechanic instantly knew he was talking about his mech. Pilots often had a habit of naming their machines to tie the bonds they shared with them. After all, operating one often gave the sensation that a Colossus's body was a natural extension of their own. It would be strange for a pilot *not* to name their mech.

Matt looked into his bag and noticed a treasure only the elites at the camp carried: smartphones, plus accompanying chargers.

"Yes, sir!" he gleefully confirmed.

He had only caught glimpses of smartphones before, often from a distance. With enough tinkering, he and his men would be able to call each other anywhere from within the facility, making work significantly more efficient.

He directed one of his top men to show the Hunter where he would be staying. The young twenty-something then escorted him to a five-story complex next to the hangar. This was where all the mechanics and pilots stayed.

"That unit's quite something! A little worse for wear, but it's practically a work of art. We don't get too many sleek models; they're all heavy-hitters. If I didn't know any better, I'd say it came directly from the W.O.D."

"Hmph."

That was all the Hunter said. The engineer could have sworn he saw a smirk on his face for just a brief second. He quickly forgot about it as they approached the man's assigned door.

Inside was something that looked more like a small walk-in closet. To the people of Nuevo Oasis, however, this was considered a high-end luxury for a single person to have all this space to themselves. Often, you would see entire families squeeze themselves into these rooms; hence, they often used these places for sleep and nothing else.

The pilot scanned what little there was to see before the young man intercepted.

"Uh, the bathroom is on the first floor; same goes for the showers."

The guest nodded in response. "Take me to the eatery. There's gotta be one here."

"Oh! Uh, this way."

The worker was taken by surprise by the sudden request. Then again, he thought, he really should not. This man must have been traversing the desert for God knows how long. Such a trip should work up a hell of an appetite.

As the chaperone guided him to their camp's cafeteria, the Hunter studied his surroundings and took in every sight. He saw numerous people moving to and from, each wearing the same gray uniform but with multicolored stripes. Those with green-striped jumpsuits carried heavy containers, some of which were labeled "FRAGILE" or "HANDLE WITH CARE." The ones with blue-striped jumpsuits carried large brown backpacks labeled "MAIL" with papers and small packages seeping out. Some also wore yellow-striped jumpsuits with mops, buckets, and gasmasks. Finally, those with red-striped jumpsuits were equipped with white duffle bags having "EMERGENCY" printed on them.

The Hunter assumed these were but a few of the numerous jobs offered within the walls of Nuevo Oasis, and that these were the occupations that required employees to constantly move from location to location.

As the pair got closer to their destination, the man also witnessed children playing outside with adult supervision, each one in a purple-striped jumpsuit. The kids played all kinds of games: jump rope, soccer, hopscotch, catch, frisbee, and hacky sack, to name a few. The preteens and teenagers were all most likely receiving their education elsewhere.

The Hunter did notice one thing in particular with everyone he saw: no one seemed to own any smart devices, nor any other kind of device that could access the Internet. He saw a few people here and there communicating with walkie-talkies or listening to music on their portable radios. It appeared that the most advanced technology that was accessible to the common folk were pre-Internet devices. He realized then that the smartphones he gave to Matt must have been worth more than he thought, and that perhaps he should not have given the mechanic so many.

Eventually, they arrived at the cafeteria where everyone got their daily portions to last throughout the day. The Hunter noticed that the young man was still by his side as he got in line.

"Aren't you gonna head back to work?"

"Uh, sorry, sir. I was instructed to stay with you for the first day of your stay," the mechanic nervously explained.

The Hunter did not say anything in response. The local could not help but wonder what exactly the Hunter was thinking. In fact, he could not get a read on him at all. Though, he was too afraid to ask what was on his mind.

The two got their rations consisting of canned fruit, canned decontaminated meat, crackers, and fresh rice. To get access to water, the young man explained, the Hunter needed to carry his own container, though he allowed him to use his. Once they seated, the Hunter looked around the numerous rows of tables.

It was the middle of the day, so naturally, the majority of the benches were filled. He could see numerous people of all different backgrounds, ages, and ethnicities. A quarter of them did not even speak English. He saw some individuals sit in isolation, several enjoying the comfort of friends, and a few with families of their own. He then looked over to his escort.

"What's your name, kid?"

"Me? Oh. It's Dave."

"Tell me, Dave, how old are you?"

"Twenty, sir."

"How long have you lived here?"

"Nuevo Oasis? Well, pretty much my whole life."

Dave tried to think back to a time when he was not within the safety of his camp's protective walls to no avail. He had been told by his parents that they were accepted into the camp when he was a baby after they had agreed to serve as sanitary workers.

"Ever piloted a Colossus?" the Hunter continued asking.

"Other than basic test drives, no. But I hope to someday! Matt says I might get a chance soon with a new model we've been working on!"

"Don't," the pilot said as he began digging into his meal.

"W-why shouldn't I? You seem to be enjoying the life. Going out there, being your own man. I heard about that giant rat you brought in. Must've been exciting, huh?"

The Hunter turned to face him and took off his sunglasses, revealing that he was blind in one eye. It was the very eye that was surrounded by his burn marks.

"It's not worth it."

Dave could swear that the blind eye was looking straight into his soul. Before he could respond, he heard a loud noise as the doors slammed open and a large burly and bearded man came swaggering in.

"I'll have the usual, gramps! A hard worker's gotta eat, ya know?" he proclaimed to the chef.

The chef sighed in frustration. "Of course, Fuego."

He provided his loud guest a gourmet meal in comparison to the rations everyone else got. As he was walking towards the tables, already eating his meatball sub, a group left their table empty for him.

"Whatever you do, don't cross Fuego. He's the head of the guards, though if you ask me, he's not that good of a pilot. He mainly relies on the newest models we build at the hangar."

The Hunter watched Fuego finish one of three sandwiches before he sat at his table, which happened to be right across from them.

"Now, let's see what we got ourselves today! Oh? Grilled chicken! Well, don't mind if I do!" Fuego boisterously proclaimed as he began scarfing down on his lunch.

"How'd this clown get to be a pilot?" the Hunter asked Dave as he noticed Fuego's rotund physic.

"No one knows, but the guys at work think he has some connection with the higher-ups who run the place."

Once Fuego finished scarfing down his poultry-filled meal, he was about to reach for his dessert until he noticed the Hunter from the corner of his eye. The large man saw something he had never seen from any of the locals -- the look of pure disdain.

"I see you lookin' at me like you're all high and mighty. You think you're better than me!" Fuego immediately stood up and lumbered over to the Hunter and Dave's table. Everyone around them got up and left immediately.

"I've never seen such a sorry excuse for a pilot in all my life," the man matter-of-factly stated.

"What?"

Fuego slammed his greasy hand on the table in an act of dominance. Dave began to move away while his acquaintance stood his ground.

"I don't think I've seen your face before."

"H-he's with me, Fuego... he's new," Dave muttered in an attempt to save himself the trouble of explaining to Matt why the man he was tasked to look after ended up in a body bag.

"New? If he's with you, then he must..." it took a while for the gears in Fuego's brain to finally turn. "Ah! So, you must be the guy who brought in that rat. Looked pretty delicious. I suppose I have to thank you for my dinner, but you can forget it!"

Fuego's voice grew louder as his already enormous ego began to expand.

"Now, normally I would beat the daylights outta ya. But since we're technically brothers in arms, I'll just take what's left of your rations. You too, boy, since you're *his* chaperone."

Fuego reached out to grab the Hunter's plate before the outsider stopped his arm with just one hand.

"You're not taking anything," he said slowly with a cold stare.

"Now you're askin' for it!" Fuego shouted as he threw a punch.

With lightning speed, the stranger jumped from his table to avoid Fuego's fist. The Hunter elbowed him in the chest before throwing in two jabs to the face. Fuego stumbled back until he hit his own table. He smeared his nose, only to find blood on his hand.

"That does it! I'm challenging you to a Death Duel!"

Everyone in the vicinity gasped in alarm. The confused Hunter looked over at his chaperone.

"Death Duel?"

"It's our way of settling scores outside of the camp without causing any civilian casualties," Dave nervously explained.

It only took the Hunter a few seconds to consider his challenger's request before coming up with an answer.

"Sure, tomorrow morning at ten."

A good chunk of the audience cheered on. The Hunter was confused by this sudden surge of energy, all while his rival chuckled.

"Good. That's about the smartest decision you've made yet. Your next will be dyin' if you know what's good for ya!"

"We gotta go!" Dave loudly told the Hunter as he pulled him out of that crowd.

Meanwhile, Fuego sat back down to enjoy his meal and embrace the cheers of the people who would no doubt support him.

As they both walked back towards the hangar, he heard all kinds of cheers and jeers from the inhabitants of the camp.

"Why is everyone excited?" asked the Hunter.

"Death Duels are the most exciting things to happen here, outside of the occasional mutant attack. But when those happen everyone bunkers down in fear and pray to whatever god that our Colossi can handle it."

"On top of that," Dave added, "it gives everyone the perfect excuse to start gambling big. Some people ride everything they have on these fights. Makes sense, really. Y'know, this camp used to be a gamblin' town. I think they called it--"

"Las Vegas. I know."

"Oh, right. You look old enough to have experienced the Age of Glory."

By the time they got back to the complex, news had already spread of the Death Duel between him and Fuego. On every monitor in the hangar's offices, there were images of the Hunter's mech, Bravura; and Fuego's powerhouse of a machine, Skullimination. The latter turned out to be the very Colossus stationed next to Bravura. All around them were photographers shoving into each other in an attempt to get the best photos of the two mechs in the hopes of selling them to the local news outlet.

The two snuck around the back to a secret entrance. Inside, Matt was there to angrily greet them.

"What the hell happened out there, Dave? I gave you one simple job and now all our work is gonna go to waste!"

"I-its not my fault, boss!" the panicked rookie explained to his superior. "Fuego tried to take our food and this guy here went all Bruce Lee on him!"

Matt pinched the bridge of his nose in exasperation. "Jesus Christ, ya had to run into that idiot."

The Hunter looked over at a nearby news monitor and noticed the stats comparison. There he saw his mech's speed, agility, durability, and strength. He rushed Matt and grabbed his neck.

"What the hell are Bravura's stats doing up there? I *paid* you!" the Hunter growled.

"I-*ack*! I had no choice!"

The Hunter threw Matt to the ground to explain.

"*Cough* It's required by the Council for visitors to have their Colossi info submitted."

The pilot was getting ready to beat the tar out of this traitor. As he approached him, Matt raised his hands while Dave was sweating a storm, thinking he was going to be next.

"W-Wait! They're fake!"

His attacker stopped dead in his tracks.

"I sent them fake stats!"

"Explain. *Now!*" the Hunter demanded.

Matt was exasperating.

"I sent them data that's similar but not exactly the same as yours. I had a few men who didn't tune up your mech create an approximation of what they thought it was capable of based on similar-looking Colossi."

The fury in the Hunter's eyes slowly faded. Meanwhile, Matt got back up off the ground and fixed his uniform.

"Don't worry, you're mech's secrets are safe with us. That being said, I gotta say, your machine is one of a kind. The things you got in store for Fuego are--"

"That's enough," the Hunter said as he cut Matt off, "I'll do this fight tomorrow and I'll be on my way."

"Wait, what!" Dave exclaimed. "Even if you do beat Fuego, which no one has, you still have a whole week here."

"It'll only be a matter of time till someone gets Bravura's data out of you and comes after me. I'm not safe here anymore."

"What do you mean?" Matt queried. "People like Fuego aren't very common. Nuevo Oasis is one of the safest camps around!"

"That's what they all say," bellowed the pilot before he left for his living quarters.

Matt and Dave looked at each other in confusion.

***

Morning arrived and the Hunter was greeted with the closest thing anyone in the camp has ever gotten to breakfast in bed in a long while. As he ate his delivered rations in his room, Matt and Dave explained to him the process of the Death Duel.

"Basically, the two of you will be taken to a safe distance away from the camp just within range of our satellites where cameras will be recording and televising the whole thing," Matt exposited.

"Your Colossu- I mean, Bravura, is ready to go, but we weren't allowed to give you any extra weapons," Dave added.

"I got plenty to work with," the Hunter responded.

"Hope you're right. It'd be a shame for a Colossus like yours to be totaled," said Matt.

"How're you not scared?" Dave asked. "Fuego's machine is a monster!"

The challenger got up and placed his sunglasses back on.

"Simple. I *hunt* monsters."

***

The morning sun rose on Nuevo Oasis. Out from the front gate were several guard units, followed by the reigning champ and the challenger. A portion of the dome opened to reveal a wide set of bleachers, packed with an abundance of locals all hyping themselves up in anticipation of the upcoming showdown. In front of them, wide screens were set up to allow a better view of what was about to take place. At that moment, several jeeps and dune buggies, each equipped with a massive camera drove out of the gate, pursuing the mechs.

Once the party of Colossi was at a safe enough distance from the camp, the guards instructed the pilots of Bravura and Skullimination to face each other. All but one of the guard units stayed with the opponents to act as a referee while the rest retreated back to the safety of their abode. The vehicles all went into their assigned positions as they circled the metal titans, ready to broadcast the carnage to the live audience and anyone in the camp that owned cable television sets.

"Alright!" the referee loudly instructed, his words broadcasting to every device in Nuevo Oasis. "I want you to give the people what they want. A no-holds-barred brawl! You may use anything and everything to beat the ever-loving hell outta each other. The victor may decide to either execute the loser or banish him. Either way, the victor will do whatever he will please with the loser's Colossus."

"Fine by me, Mr. Ref!" Fuego smirked. "I enjoy playing for keeps."

The Hunter said nothing and had his machine nod its head in approval to the referee's demands.

Matt, along with Dave and the rest of his subordinates, were seated in the back row of the bleachers. In his hands was a portable television that could switch between each camera. Such a luxury was only given to the very people that worked to keep Nuevo Oasis's last line of defense in operation. Everyone else was forced to watch whatever camera angles the broadcasters believed were the most exciting.

On the corner of every screen, Matt noticed the name "Hunter" listed as the visitor's name.

"'Hunter?' Was this your idea?" the man asked his protégé.

"H-he never gave us his name," Dave hesitantly replied, "that was the best I could come up with. So, you think he's gonna be alright?"

"Hard to tell, Dave," Matt postulated "His machine's pretty special, but it'll take more than that to take care of Fuego."

"Special? Looks to me like a standard soldier unit from the war."

"You'll see, kid," Matt said under his breath as he smiled.

Dave could tell his boss was excited.

"Let's get this party started already!" Fuego impatiently shouted.

The big bearded champion was almost giddy to destroy the man who had soiled his reputation as the toughest, most dangerous man alive.

The referee's mech moved back past the circle of cameramen. Once the ref determined that he was at a far enough distance, his Colossus raised its mechanical arms.

"Ready… get set… *obliterate!*"

Fuego's bot came in swinging with a barrage of heat-seeking missiles from its massive shoulders.

The Hunter went right to work as he manipulated his Colossus into swerving around every missile as each one missed him and exploded into the ground. Bravura proved to be remarkably agile, as it avoided every projectile, jumping and running circles around Skullimination.

"Pretty fancy feet you got there," Fuego remarked. "Let's see you dodge this!"

Fuego activated a panel on Skullimination's right leg that opened to reveal a large gun. His mech pulled it out from its slot and began firing crimson red beams of plasma energy at his opponent.

Once more, Bravura bobbed and weaved through every devastating shot. Meanwhile, the vehicles on the ground scrambled around the two contestants as they tried to record the fight from the finest angles possible. The crew with the best live footage would be granted an amazing bonus that would set them practically for the rest of the year within the camp. To them, such a reward was absolutely worth risking their lives over.

Unfortunately, one film crew, a rather inexperienced one, paid the ultimate price when a shot from Skullimination's plasma rifle blasted them to smithereens.

"Hold still, dammit!"

Fuego was getting annoyed. He made sure to pack his weapons with enough ammo to wipe out a small platoon of soldier units like Bravura. Yet, his weapons could not land on his swift target. It did not help matters that his target's massive cloth made it impossible to see its individual limbs in action.

Just then, Bravura came close enough to land one jab to Skullimination's torso and another to the face. Fuego was caught completely off guard.

"What the--? Why, you!"

Fuego activated another panel, this time on his Colossus's left leg. Out came a wide serrated sword. Fuego made sure to have his metal puppet swing its weapon with all its might. Bravura had managed to avoid getting hit, with its blade slicing the end of his cloak. More rips to add to the collection of tears and holes.

"Heh, you can't keep running away forever. Either give up now and face your death, or I'ma have to get real nasty!" Fuego stated with a disgusting grin. "And by nasty, I mean torturing ya for as long as possible! For some reason, people seem to misinterpret that."

As Fuego was distracting himself with his own monologue, the Hunter pressed a large button on his control panel. Attached to each of the robot's forearms was a black module attachment. The right module had "Bravura" inscribed in old chipped paint, while the left one had the same alpha/omega insignia the pilot had tattooed on his shoulder. Fastened to the right compartment were two metal rods. As soon as Bravura pulled one of them off, the pressure-sensitive pole extended out on both sides, with each end crackling with electricity.

"Huh? So, ya got yourself some toys to play with as well," Fuego mentioned. "This oughta be fun!"

Skullimination rushed into battle while wildly swinging its blade in every direction. As Bravura moved side to side it would counter any attacks that came within centimeters with its mechanical bo staff. The slender contraption twirled around its rod in a display that left Fuego absolutely confounded. He could not tell where his enemy's attack would come from until it was too late.

Bravura slammed its weapon into Skullimination's legs multiple times, bringing the behemoth to its knees. From there, the cloaked figure thrust one of the electrical ends of the staff into the right shoulder of the hulking figure, causing this part of the mech to burst in an array of fire and shrapnel. Skullimination's arm was left dangling, completely useless, with its rifle dropping to the ground.

The Hunter proceeded to bash Fuego's mech, rattling him inside in the process.

"Ah! You think you've won just because you know a few moves? Well, I got a trick up my sleeve too!"

Fuego activated a switch in his cockpit. His mech's visor glowed green, along with the panel linings of its large antennae. The Hunter knew this was not a good sign, but before he could finish off his opponent, Fuego kept him at a safe enough distance with his razor-sharp instrument of destruction.

The Hunter's radar detected three massive objects off in the distance beyond the dome. They were approaching, and fast. The terrible trio, spherical in nature, had rolled onto the battlefield, destroying a number of vehicles in the process. The referee himself panicked as the entities grew ever closer. He aimed his Colossus's hand cannons at one of the mysterious bodies and shot wildly at it.

His actions, however, only spelled his doom as the heavily armored orb proved too strong for his weapon to inflict much damage. The object uncurled to reveal itself as a mutant with razor-sharp claws, a spiked tail, and an armored snout filled with gruesome teeth. This rabid creature had to have been an armadillo in a past life, the Hunter thought.

He, Fuego, and the residents of Nuevo Oasis watching and listening in on the fight could hear the referee screaming for his life as the large rodent mauled him, ripping his Colossus to shreds until it burst into flames like a landmine. The creature howled, unfazed by the detonation, and seemingly unsatisfied with its hollow victory.

The Hunter was greatly disturbed by the man's screams as sweat rolled down his forehead. Memories of battles long ago rushed to the forefront of his mind. He could hear dozens of familiar screams… the screams of ghosts calling out to him. His hands shook as fear's grip grew ever tighter around his mind.

Just then, another giant orb was heading in his direction. The Hunter snapped out of his dark trance and was forced to repel the unveiled attacker with his bo staff. The creature uncurled and launched at Bravura. The moment the electric tip made contact with the approaching force's stomach he could hear the beast make high-pitched shrills. It appeared that their undersides were sensitive to electricity.

As the second mutant retreated, another popped up from behind to catch Bravura off guard. Luckily, the Hunter was no longer distracted by phantoms of the past. His dulled mind sharpened once more. He moved out of the way and witnessed the third attacker curl back into a ball. From his speakers, he could hear the growing chuckles of the obese scoundrel.

"You better watch your back, Hunter! They haven't had a good meal in a while. You could say they're a little antsy. Heh, I know the feeling."

Immediately, the three mutants closed in on Bravura in all directions. It was then that the cornered pilot realized the glutton was distracting him. He had Bravura activate the compartment around its left arm. The mechanical module unfolded into a shield that surged with electricity. Bravura then raised the shield to the mutant to his left while aiming both ends of its staff to the mutants in front and behind. The Hunter could feel the impact of all three beasts, but due to their armored hides, the creatures were not detracted by the electricity. If only he had access to their underbellies like last time.

The trio of monsters continued to push forward and claw at the mech with ghastly snarls and growls. Their increased size and bulk was like a throwback to their prehistoric ancestors, as if the radiation had unlocked recessive genes that remained dormant for millions of years. However, unlike their ancient predecessors, these animals appeared to be both carnivorous and feral.

"Heh heh heh. You enjoying my babies' company? They sure like *you*," Fuego gloated.

Despite his opponent being preoccupied in a life-or-death situation, the egotistical brute had Skullimination point to its antennae with its remaining hand as if the Hunter could still see him.

"Made this device of mine shortly after the war. I use a special frequency to tap into my mutants' hearing and direct them to any target I so choose. When I ain't fighting, I use a different one to keep them away from the camp. Now, anyone who messes with me will receive the wrath of my Hellhogs! Though I never had to use them until now."

Back in the bleachers, Dave and the rest of his colleagues were drenched in sweat. Meanwhile, his superior looked as cool as a cucumber as he remained expressionless. His eyes were closely focused on Bravura on his portable screen.

"How could the higher-ups allow this?" Dave asked. "That's cheating, isn't it?"

"Did you forget that this is a no-holds-barred fight to the death?" Matt replied. "Anything and everything is possible. Once a Death Duel is established, each fighter is allowed to bring whatever he needs to win. This is just something no one's ever used before. Now I see why Fuego always got special treatment."

"What do you mean?" questioned Dave.

"Think about it. With that kind of tech the camp will no longer have to worry about mutants ever again."

"That's good, right?"

"In theory, yes," answered Matt. "But something doesn't sit right with me."

"Whaddya mean, chief?" another subordinate asked. Dave himself was just about to ask the same thing.

"Think about it. If the Council had access to that technology all this time, why didn't they reveal its existence? We wouldn't have to worry about any more mutant attacks."

"Maybe the tech's not perfected," Dave suggested. "Maybe it only works on those things."

"Nah, if that were the case, the announcement would've at least boosted the morale of everyone here at the camp. No, they probably wanted to keep this a secret as a means of developing it even further. Create something that could potentially control the minds of more complex animals."

"Complex?" Dave repeated as the gears turned in his head. "Complex, like…" His eyes widened in horror. "Humans."

"Bingo."

All around Matt were the gasps of his men. Several audience participants overheard them and began eavesdropping out of morbid curiosity.

"Right now, I bet our dear leaders are pretty pissed off at Fuego for ruining their surprise," Matt continued. "Then again, I wouldn't trust a loudmouth like Fuego to begin with, so I'd say it's their fault for thinking he could ever be discreet."

Back in the desert, Bravura's strength was pushed to its very limits. Its mechanical servos and pistons that fueled the resistance were straining to the point of collapsing as the Hellhogs pushed ever so closely. With no other option, the Hunter resorted to his final option.

Towards the edge of his control panel were two devices resembling arcade joysticks of the 1990s laying on their sides away from him. The pilot took off his sunglasses, set them aside, and pulled a lever below the panel towards him. This activated the joysticks to stand upwards. He quickly grabbed both and slid them towards him along a set path until they were locked into position. This, in turn, activated a special helmet to lower from the ceiling of the cockpit to fit over his head.

Outside the cockpit, the blue visor that represented Bravura's face shut down. Just then, the armored plates that protected its forehead head shifted forward over its face. The two halves combined, activating a center crest to slide up and reveal two spaces that gave the appearance of eyeholes.

Bravura's visor then ignited through the eyeholes of its new faceplate with a bright crimson light. Using its new set of eyes, the mech quickly surveyed the scene. Upon finding an opening overhead, the Colossus jumped over its enemies, with all three Hellhogs crashing into each other.

Everyone, including Fuego, was stunned at the unexpected escape.

"I don't know what's goin' on with that mech of yours, but it's gonna take more than a silly mask to get rid of my babies!"

Bravura leaped off one of the creature's bony carapace and sprinted towards Skullimination. Trailing behind were the rolling Hellhogs, determined to run over their prey. Panicking, Fuego ordered his machine to drop its sword and reclaim its rifle. He fired wildly into Bravura's direction. The robot warrior swayed left and right, perfectly dodging every shot.

But unlike prior evasions, Bravura was still on the offense as it closed the gap between the two mechs. All the while, the armored mutants were trailing after Bravura. Several of Fuego's shots landed on the lead Hellhog. Even its mutated carapace was not enough to survive mankind's horrific technology. Its corpse uncurled and crashed into the ground.

"Damn you! How dare you make me shoot one of my own! You owe me a new mutant!"

With Bravura within striking distance, Skullimination swung its only arm, rifle in hand, at its opponent. With such frighteningly perfect timing, Bravura ducked underneath at the last second, nearly missing the long reach of the black Colossus and sprinted past him.

"Hey, where are you runnin' off to, coward?" screamed Fuego before noticing the sounds of the Hellhogs approaching.

Unfortunately for him, his reaction speed was nowhere near as quick as the Hunter's as he was trampled over by the ferocious *cingulatas*.

Over at the bleachers, the crowd grew wild at Bravura's stunning comeback, while others moaned and dreaded at the realization of their lost bets.

"What the heck's going on with his Colossus?" Dave finally asked his boss. "I've never heard of any soldier unit with such reaction speed!"

"That's because it's no ordinary soldier unit," Matt said with a grin, excited to finally reveal his secret. "Having been the only person to inspect the machine firsthand, I can tell you that Colossus you see before you was one of the greatest technological marvels to ever come out of the War of Desolation... the Atlus!"

"What's so special about the Atlus?" one of his men asked.

"The Atlus units were designed to be the cream of the crop!" Matt shouted, his excitement getting the best of him. "I always wanted to see one with my own eyes."

"As you've probably noticed," Matt further exposited as he pointed to his screen, "the visor has been completely covered by this new mask. A normal Colossus visor can give pilots a wide range of vision. But once this system is activated its vision becomes as sharp as a hawk. By limiting its range, an Atlus can zero in on any target and process when and where to strike, dodge, and react with impeccable timing.

"At the same time, the user's controls also become limited to only the most essential movements required for fighting and nothing more. The only downside is that with so much focus on one target at a time, it becomes very easy to ambush it in the event of multiple targets. The fact that our Hunter here is using it in a four-on-one match is an achievement in itself."

As the mechanic gushed over his appreciation for this instrument of war, the Hunter was continuing to run further away from Fuego. Once the repugnant pilot got his mech back on its damaged feet, he amped up his radio frequency to its highest level.

"Eviscerate the Hunter, my babies! Make sure nothing remains!"

Skullimination's antennae vibrated more intensely, and the Hellhogs' ferocity grew evermore rabid. Once the Hunter heard these words, he turned Bravura around to face the approaching creatures.

Through his visor, the pilot concentrated on Skullimination's wide frame and nothing else. The Colossus's shield folded back into its compartment. It raised its staff over its shoulder like an Olympic javelin thrower.

Closer and closer the mutant armadillos got, their mouths now salivating with the thought of feasting upon the innards of their metal foe. They were too blinded by rage to roll into their globular forms as they were running wildly at their prey. Fuego grinned, thinking his opponent had lost his mind. To the mutant wrangler, the fight was his.

The moment of truth arrived. Bravura threw the pole with as much force as it could muster. The electrical staff sped between both mutants, who failed to even notice the weapon.

Fuego witnessed the approaching projectile and attempted to move out of the way. The pole grazed his robot's head, shattering its right antennae to pieces.

"Ha! Ya missed, idiot. This duel is mine. No one messes with Fuego!"

However, his Hellhogs did not finish the job as they initially intended. They slowed to a crawl as they approached Bravura. The pair seemed lost, confused, aimless. Realizing this, the Hunter breathed an exhausted sigh of relief.

"What the hell are ya doin'? Kill the bastard! Rip him to shreds!" Fuego shouted.

He attempted to adjust the frequency to an even higher setting. Just then, sparks flew from his Colossus's head. The Hellhogs' sensitive ears picked up on the new sound, but this one was unfamiliar to them. It caused the armored creatures an immense amount of discomfort, but this time they were able to determine the source: it was the black monolith that was right behind them.

They turned around, their rage returned in full force as they began spinning towards their master.

"Hey, w-w-what are you two doing? Doncha recognize me?" Fuego's voice trembled as he uttered those last words.

The besieged champion looked over to his rifle, which had been smashed to pieces by the mutants and checked his surroundings until he saw his sword at a distance. He attempted to walk towards his blade before his mech's damaged legs buckled under the enormous weight of the machine's upper half.

The man who at one point considered himself the king of Nuevo Oasis turned to look at the misfortune he had created for himself. All sense of confidence and ego was nowhere to be seen as he whimpered and pleaded for his opponent to save him.

"Ya gotta save me, Hunter! I'll give you anything. I'll give you my Colossus, my weapons, whatever you want!"

Unfortunately for Fuego, the man had already begun to leave the scene, uttering only one single request:

"I want you to suffer."

It was a request he most definitely got as he heard Fuego's hysterical cries for several minutes before he was abruptly silenced in an explosion. Once the Hellhogs finished digging through their victim's metal corpse, they began to migrate deep into the desert, never to be seen again.

***

As the sun began to set the large community of Nuevo Oasis citizens gathered around the hangar to bid their visitor farewell. Inside, the mechanics each provided rations to the Hunter, who respectfully and quietly accepted them. He was approached by Matt, who just completed the last of Bravura's repairs.

"She's good for now, but given the way you fight, it'll only be a matter of time 'til she needs another check-up. However, I did throw in something that'll help you with that. Consider it a thank you for exposing Fuego."

A small smile formed on the Hunter's face. The mechanic held out his hand, and he, in turn, reached out and shook it. As the Hunter was about to board the platform that would lift him to his cockpit, Dave appeared out of the crowd of employees.

"Hold on! Why do you have to go? We still need you! What if something happens and the Council tries to mind control us or something?"

The Hunter knew full well what the young man was talking about, having been filled in on Fuego's now lost tech and its dark implications by Matt the night before. It was only a matter of time until the corrupt leaders of Nuevo Oasis chased him down for causing them so much trouble. They were most likely waiting for him to leave as killing off the popular champion would not be a good look for the Council. There was also the matter of Bravura's own unique mechanisms, something many would surely want to get their hands on after seeing it in action.

On top of it all, he was done helping others. Those days were far behind him, as he had his own matters to attend to. Yet, deep down, the Hunter felt obligated to leave the boy, and everyone, with a parting gift of his own. He breathed in and let out a long sigh.

"If something happens to me, what will you do then? How long do you think you'll last?"

Dave was silent. The pilot took off his sunglasses as he stared at him.

"If the people of Nuevo Oasis can't help themselves," the Hunter continued, "then it isn't a place worth keeping."

The man turned around and stepped aboard the platform. Off he went as he rose above everyone in silence. The Hunter entered his cockpit and gazed at the folks that took him in. He waited until the door fully closed before he put back on his sunglasses.

The massive gates opened, and Bravura marched out. The Hunter checked his systems and noticed an old monitor that had been deactivated for quite some time switching on. He let out a small chuckle.

The warrior eventually walked out of the main gates of Nuevo Oasis with a crowd of people cheering him on. Once he was a mile away, his radar detected a four-man squad of security units trailing behind him. It was the guards, waiting for him to leave the safety of the camp and the public eye.

"Stop right there! You're under arrest by the order of the Council of Nuevo Oasis!"

The Hunter smiled and flipped a dusty switch.

"Let's see what this baby can do."

The Colossus's back ignited with burning fuel due to a newly installed jetpack. It was one that allowed Bravura to move at greater speeds, easily able to outrun the guards as its enormous body lifted off the ground.

By the time Matt and his team reached the open gates, their guest was disappearing into the distance. Matt could tell Dave was still worried and placed his hand on his apprentice's shoulder.

"He was right, you know. It's not his place to clean up our mistakes. We allowed things to get this bad, right under our noses. Got too complacent with the way things were. It's our responsibility to keep Nuevo Oasis in shape, otherwise it's 'Desolation' all over again."

"What do you think'll happen to him?" Dave asked.

"Him? Oh, he'll do what he does best," Matt said with a smile. "Something we could all learn to do:

"Survive."

END

ABOUT THE AUTHOR

Andres Perez is a Japan-based English teacher and aspiring film critic who makes reviews and podcasts covering movies, television, comics, and games on his YouTube channel KaijuNoir. He is also a freelance editor who has worked on other projects such as the giant monster comic *Nagoraiar: Against the Terror of the Moon* as well as the mythology-themed novel *Gods' Wrath: Tournament of the Divine Book I.*

ABOUT THE ARTISTS

Larry Quach

Larry Quach is a concept artist/illustrator living in Los Angeles that works in the entertainment industry. Since 2011 after graduating from Art Center College of design, he has worked in film, games, mobile games, and theme parks. He enjoys illustrating Kaiju for fun and enjoys selling his artwork at various conventions.

Tyler Sowles

Tyler Sowles is an indie comic illustrator with a love for monsters and dinosaurs. He has published material through Arcana (*The Numbered*) and Source Point Press (*Hank Steiner: Monster Detective*; *FallStreak*), as well as self-published his own work (*Durontus: The Lost Serpent*).

Lungga Creatives: (in alphabetical order)

Elden Ardiente

Jimi Bautista

Jim Faustino

Glenn Lugapo

Ferdie Misa

Benjamin Quinajon

We are a virtual creative studio with a focus on illustration, story art, concept art, and book cover designs. For more info and to see our sample works, visit us on Facebook: @lunggacreatives.

In a world of Divine Beings and Beasts...
The Gods will show their WRATH!

GODS' WRATH
Tournament of the Divine
Written by William T. Kearney

Available on Amazon!

Follow on
Youtube: Crookedlore Productions
Facebook: Crookedlore

155

Printed in Great Britain
by Amazon